LOVE IN LUGANO

Suzannah Lloyd, sculptor and horticulturist, arrives at an exhibition in
Lugano which is showing some of
her orchid sculptures. There she
meets Mr Di Stefano, who offers her
a job managing the grounds of his
estate and orchid collection. Working
closely with Mr Di Stefano's right
hand man, Dante Candurro, she
falls in love with him — but
overhears his plans to steal the Di
Stefano art collection. Feeling
betrayed by further deception, can
she ever learn to trust him?

ANNE CULLEN

◆

LOVE IN LUGANO

Complete and Unabridged

LINFORD
Leicester

First published in Great Britain in 2007

First Linford Edition
published 2008

Copyright © 2007 by Anne Cullen

British Library CIP Data

Cullen, Anne
    Love in Lugano.—Large print ed.—
Linford romance library
    1. Love stories
    2. Large type books
    I. Title
    823.9'2 [F]

    ISBN 978–1–84782–104–1

Published by
F. A. Thorpe (Publishing)
Anstey, Leicestershire

Set by Words & Graphics Ltd.
Anstey, Leicestershire
Printed and bound in Great Britain by
T. J. International Ltd., Padstow, Cornwall

This book is printed on acid-free paper

1

'I can't believe you did this, Suzannah. I thought you had better judgement,' said Dante Candurro, with barely concealed anger.

Suzannah Lloyd straightened up and resolved not to be intimidated by Dante, her boss, Mr Di Stefano's right hand man.

'You left me in charge and gave me a completely free hand. That area of land was an overgrown mess and now it isn't. I thought Mr Di Stefano would like an alpine rockery. I worked damn hard to finish it before you got back. If I was supposed to leave that area alone, you should have been clearer about my remit before you left on your trip,' said Suzannah.

'Can't you see . . . '

' . . . Let me finish, Dante. That area was choking with weeds and the bushes were in danger of overtaking the whole estate. I checked all the species of plants that were growing there before I did anything and I didn't pull out anything rare.

They were just weeds that were taking light from the greenhouses,' said Suzannah.

'But now the area is cleared, can't you see that this area is a security risk for the whole estate?'

'And it wasn't before?' said Suzannah, defiantly.

Dante hesitated a moment, 'No it wasn't,' he said eventually. 'The greenhouses weren't visible to anyone snooping around the perimeter fence and now thanks to you they are.'

Suzannah could feel the colour flush in her cheeks, as she realised what Dante was getting at.

Although no one had told her specifically about security, she knew she should have guessed. People as wealthy as Mr Di Stefano always had to worry about personal security, she knew she should have guessed. People as wealthy as Mr Di Stefano always had to worry about personal security, particularly with the world-famous Di Stefano sculpture collection to consider, which although housed in an unknown location, was popularly thought to be stored somewhere on this estate, as well as his beloved and unique orchid collection, carefully cultivated in the greenhouses.

'Dante, I see what you mean. Maybe I was wrong, but you must understand that even before I tore out all that shrubbery, a child could climb over the perimeter fence; it isn't even alarmed.

A bit of greenery wouldn't deter professional thieves, in fact if anyone entered the estate they could have used those shrubs as cover, now they can't. Look, I know Switzerland is a low risk crime area, but even so . . . '

Suzannah looked at the Dante's furious brown eyes and hesitated, biting back tears. Realising further conversation was pointless, she turned round and walked back to the house, ignoring her name being called after her. I knew this job was all too good to be true, she thought as she stole a glance at the magnificent grounds that had recently become her home.

Suzannah's initial upset turned to anger. He didn't want me here from the start. Dante was just looking for an excuse, thought Suzannah, as she realised Dante, was more often than not cold towards her, in contrast to the one occasion she met Mr Di Stefano, who couldn't have been friendlier.

Dante was a mystery to Suzannah; he never offered anything in the way of personal information and conversation was always restricted to work. Dante was also, however, the right hand man of a very wealthy businessman — Mr Di Stefano, Suzannah's employer. He probably saw me as a threat, thought Suzannah angrily, fuming at Dante's attitude.

Once back in her room, Suzannah locked her door and looked out of the window for what she assumed would be the last time and gazed out across the magnificent turquoise of Lake Lugano and at the snow-capped peaks in the distance; the tranquillity of the scene was in sharp contrast to her inner turmoil.

'Ah well, I was beginning to miss the UK, anyway,' said Suzannah to herself, as she lifted down her suitcase from the top of the wardrobe and began to pack her clothes and thought about how much her life had changed over the last few weeks and wondered, unhappily where it all went wrong.

★ ★ ★

Suzannah first met her future employers one month previously, quite by chance. Some of Suzannah's work formed part of an exhibition of contemporary British sculpture in Lugano, a place with a strong tradition of visual arts and of sculpture in particular and she travelled to Switzerland to meet a number of people, connected with the exhibition and hopefully to sell some of it.

Suzannah Lloyd's skills were unusually varied. As well as being a sculptor, she had managed to support herself in a precarious artistic career by working as a horticulturist. She was equally happy when working either as an artist or with plants and she was passionate about both.

Within two hours of arriving in Lugano, Suzannah had fallen in love with the place and had been awed by the natural beauty of this Swiss lakeside city, which was situated close to the Italian border, with the alps in the distance.

It was also home to a large number of sculptures, crafted by such famous names as Giacometti and Pomodoro, that were seamlessly integrated into the town itself; around every corner was a piazza or a fountain containing a sculpture and here art was very much an everyday pleasure, for everyone.

The city also had several extensive

and beautiful public gardens and to Suzannah, Lugano seemed like heaven. This was Suzannah's first trip to Switzerland, although she knew Italy quite well and returned there for holidays to practice her Italian.

Her first impression of this Italian-speaking quarter of Switzerland was favourable. Although she recognised some close similarities with its close neighbour, the food in particular was typical of northern Italian cuisine, there were distinctive differences and the place combined the best of two different cultures in a unique way.

The exhibition, which included some of Suzannah's work, was displayed in a large privately-owned gallery. The evening before the exhibition officially opened would be the most crucial in terms of making an impression, as there was to be a large private gathering of specially-invited VIPs who would pre-view the exhibition, before it went on public display.

Suzannah understood that the invited

guests were people who knew a lot about art — collectors, curators and critics. Although the publicity would be good, Suzannah, along with most of her colleagues hoped to be able to sell some of their work and also to further their reputation in a discerning market.

Although a make or break exhibition, when the evening of the previews finally arrived, Suzannah was more excited than nervous and left plenty of time to get ready, beginning with a relaxing soak in the bath. After which, she put on an aqua silk dress, specially bought for the occasion.

After trying on several pieces of jewellery, she decided to accessorise it simply, with drop-pearl earrings and a mother of pearl brooch.

Suzannah checked her make up and brushed her long wavy, sandy hair. Just when she thought she was ready, she heard a knock at her hotel room door.

'Avanti!'

'What?' said Mark 'Mac' MacKenzie, as he came in.

'Sorry, it means come in.'

'Wow! You look fantastic, Suzannah.'

'Thanks, Mac.'

'I'm really glad you're here. None of the other Brits know any Italian, even our agent. It's lucky for us we've got you with us to translate.'

'I'll do what I can to help. I need the practice, actually, it's a while since I spoke any . . . '

' . . . What's the matter?' said Mac, wondering what had distracted Suzannah.

'Oh Mac, I'm sorry. I hoped you don't mind me mentioning this, but in this part of the world people dress a bit more formally. Do you have anything to wear other than jeans? I don't mean a suit or anything just something a little smarter.'

Mac looked down at his shabby attire. 'I see what you mean, next to you I look a bit of a tramp, but I didn't bring much with me. Besides I'm an artist, I'm supposed to look eccentric.'

'You think so?'

'No. You're right. I didn't think,' said Mac, anxiously.

Suzannah looked at the clock. 'Look, we've got plenty of time, why don't we go back to your room and see what other clothes you've got.'

'Would you?' said Mac.

'Don't worry, I'm sure we can do something,' said Suzannah, as she picked up her travel-iron and headed off determinedly to Mac's room.

Half an hour later, Mac did indeed looked more suitably dressed for the occasion in black trousers, a freshly-ironed deep purple shirt and newly-polished shoes.

Suzannah left his hair a little dishevelled, as when she tried to do something with the thick, black wiry hair, it didn't seem to look right and Suzannah conceded that anything other than a little messy just didn't look like Mac, and she had no wish to make her friend look like someone else - just a smarter, more professional version of himself.

'There. What do you think?' said Suzannah. Mac screwed up his eyes, looking at himself in the mirror.

'You've done a good job. I owe you one.'

'Anytime,' said Suzannah.

'I suppose it's time to go,' said Mac.

'You look worried,' said Suzannah.

'I am, how come you're so calm?'

'I'm excited, I'm looking forward to it all, really. I think this evening is going to be lots of fun. Anyway, let's go,' said Suzannah.

The gallery welcomed its specially-invited guests with canapés and champagne and Mac stuck close to Suzannah, while she mingled, introducing Mac and talking about the sculptures in effortless Italian.

An American lady took particular interest in Mac's small statues in soapstone and he was delighted that not only did someone love his work, but ideally, that someone spoke English.

Suzannah stood in the background, curious to see if the lady bought any of

11

Mac's work, but was soon distracted when she noticed two men, impeccably dressed in dark suits, admiring a piece of her work: a painted clay orchid.

Suzannah watched them a moment. The taller of the two was dark haired, with intense brown eyes who looked at her sculpture with brooding concentration. Suzannah thought he had the type of expression that was impossible to tell what he was thinking or even if he was happy or sad. In contrast the shorter man had a warm open face, with light brown hair and golden, slightly-freckled skin. Both men seemed to be looking at her work with more than casual interest. Ah well, here goes, thought Suzannah.

'Do you like it?' said Suzannah.

The shorter of the two men smiled warmly at Suzannah and replied, 'Very much.' Suzannah smiled and looked at the other taller man for a reaction, but none was forthcoming.

'I'm Suzannah Lloyd, this is my work. I work mainly with metal, but I also like clay, although this is a medium I've only recently started to explore.' Suzannah noticed the smaller man nod encouragingly, as she spoke, although the taller man still didn't say anything.

'I started using clay, as I have a passion for flowers and orchids in particular and this medium lends itself very well this time.' Suzannah saw the two men look at each other and wondered if she'd said something strange. The tall, mysterious man came forward to shake Suzannah's hand and said, 'My name is Dante Candurro and this is Mr Di Stefano,' indicating to the smaller man with the warm smile. 'I'm Mr Di Stefano's personal assistant.'

'The Mr Di Stefano,' repeated Suzannah, trying not to sound too overawed. The smaller man looked a little embarrassed.

'I saw some of your famous collection when it went on tour to London a couple of years ago,' said Suzannah.

'I hate to keep things of beauty locked away for too long and am happy to loan things out, as long as the galleries have adequate security, obviously.'

'I know you said you liked my work, but I would very much like your honest opinion,' asked Suzannah. Mr Di Stefano looked at Dante briefly before replying.

'I think your work shows great promise. I know from the programme, you specialise in metalwork, but personally I prefer your clay work. I think your love of flowers really comes across well in this medium,' said Mr Di Stefano.

'Thank you,' said Suzannah. 'My love of plants is more than a casual interest. I trained as a horticulturist, as well as an artist, and have worked with plants for several years. I'm equally happy with both areas and besides, it's hard to support yourself as an artist and I've found the combination of the two ideal.'

'How unusual,' said Mr Di Stefano and encouraged her to talk about her work in more detail.

Suzannah explained some of the horticultural projects she undertook in a national park and of how she developed a love for orchids from her late father, himself a keen gardener.

She found Mr Di Stefano incredibly easy to talk to and was delighted to learn that he too shared a passion for orchids and was more than a little surprised when he told her of the rare varieties he was able to cultivate in greenhouses on his nearby estate.

The comfortable ease Suzannah felt when talking to Mr Di Stefano, was in stark contrast to the quiet indifference of Dante, who hovered in the background and didn't say anything, but whose watchful eyes seemed to register everything and everyone.

There was something about him that both fascinated and unnerved her. What, she didn't know. After a few minutes, she decided he was probably rather rude and thought it a little strange that someone like Mr Di Stefano would employ someone with such an obvious lack of social skills.

'I think your boyfriend might be looking for you,' said Dante at last.

'My boyfriend?' said Suzannah puzzled. Looking round she caught Mac's eye who gave her a big grin and a thumbs up.

'That's Mac, Mark MacKenzie, some of his work's here too,' said Suzannah, trying not to let her annoyance show. 'We're just good friends.' Suzannah bit her lip and wished she hadn't said that. She knew Dante's words were rude and she reacted.

'I apologise. It's just that all the time you were talking to Mr Di Stefano, I couldn't help notice that he couldn't take his eyes off you and I assumed . . . '

'Dante. What were you thinking,' said Mr Di Stefano. 'I must apologise for Dante. Now, I will be purchasing this clay orchid, Suzannah, but on two conditions.'

Suzannah felt a twinge of nervousness on hearing this.

'Go on,' she urged.

'One, you do some more work in clay. I would really like to see you develop this aspect of your work.'

'And two . . .

'I'd very much like to show you my orchid collection. I hope it will inspire you and I want to see the results.'

'But Mr Di Stefano . . . ' said Dante, clearly horrified at what his boss had suggested.

'Yes Dante?' said Mr Di Stefano, firmly.

'Nothing, sir. I'll make the arrangements. Don't forget you have a plane to catch in an hour, sir.'

'Have the car brought round.'

'Yes, sir.' Once Dante had left to get the car, Suzannah breathed a sigh of relief.

'Thank you so much for taking an interest in my work, Mr Di Stefano. I'm delighted to have met you. I can't help but feel your right hand man perhaps doesn't like me very much.'

'Who Dante? Take no notice. He's

like that with everyone. Don't let him bother you. I don't employ him for his skills in social conversation.'

Good job you don't, thought Suzannah.

'PR isn't his strong point, but he's a brilliant lawyer and businessman, although don't tell him I said so,' said Mr Di Stefano, with a wink. 'I travel a lot on business and I need someone as astute and trustworthy as Dante to take care of my business and estate.

'You have to understand it's his job to be very security conscious. That's why he noticed your friend, looking closely in our direction. If anyone seems to take any interest in me, Dante tends to want to know exactly who that person is and will be blunt about finding out.'

'I see,' said Suzannah, trying to understand.

'Now, I have to go away on business for a few weeks, but Dante will show you round the estate, very soon and I'll be in touch.'

Even several minutes after Mr Di Stefano had left, Suzannah was still a little awestruck, as she thought of her extraordinary evening and the fact that she had sold a piece of her work. Not just a piece, but her own personal favourite and was delighted at Mr Di Stefano's suggestion of doing more flower-inspired work.

'You catching flies.'

'What? Oh Mac, you're impossible. How did you get on with the American lady, Mrs Baxter wasn't it?'

'Quite well. She bought the lot.'

'Oh Mac, that's wonderful!' said Suzannah and gave her friend a hug.

'Mrs Baxter told me you were talking to none other than The Mr Di Stefano.'

'I know, he's really friendly and do you know he's as passionate about orchids as he is about art?'

'You sound perfect for each other. You should marry him.'

'Mac! What are you talking about? Besides, I'm sure he's married with lots of children already.'

'That's not what I've heard. I'm sure he's single. They say he likes his privacy too much to let anyone get close to him.'

'That's odd, he seemed open enough to me,' said Suzannah.

'Chatty?' said Mac. 'Well I've heard that Mr Di Stefano isn't really a chatty person and if you two hit it off like that . . . '

'Stop it. Mr Di Stefano's very nice, but I certainly don't feel anything romantic for him. Besides, his Rottweiller doesn't like me.'

'Rottweiller?' said Mac, perplexed.

'Dante Candurro, his personal assistant.'

'Ah. Now I understand, well, you're not surprised that a powerful businessman like Mr Di Stefano has protective people around him, are you?'

'No, I suppose it's his job to be suspicious. Still, there was something intense about him, it was in his eyes. He completely unnerved me.'

2

The call from Dante came within a week and Suzannah was determined to enjoy the rare opportunity to look round the Di Stefano estate, regardless of Dante's attitude. Suzannah felt a twinge of excitement when she woke up that morning and quickly dressed and practically ran out of the hotel.

Once out in the sunshine, Suzannah walked over to the funicular railway, which was situated at the bottom of a mountain and watched the morning sunlight sparkle on Lake Lugano, as she waited for the squat train, that seemed more like a cable-car, to arrive. A perfect spring morning, she said to herself.

The view from the railway was amazing. Suzannah had never been on a funicular railway before and found the steepness of the journey a little scary, but it was the perfect way to enjoy the view of the city and the lake, as she was transported up the steep mountainside.

The rail journey didn't take long, and on disembarking Suzannah saw Dante waiting for her. Suzannah smiled and to her surprise he smiled back, but it was almost as if he didn't mean to, for his face quickly returned to a more familiar sombre expression.

'Thank you for meeting me.'

'No problem, Miss Lloyd.'

'Please call me Suzannah.'

Dante opened the passenger door of the four-by-four vehicle for Suzannah and they drove off, along a narrow winding road. On the journey, the lake was still visible down to their right and Suzannah watched it in silence.

After travelling five minutes, Suzannah noticed that there were gradually fewer and fewer houses and eventually, they reached some imposing wrought-iron gates. Suzannah guessed they'd arrived.

'Here we are,' said Dante, as he got

out a remote control to open the gates. 'The estate extends from the fir trees you can see on your left, right down to the lake, where we have an entrance only accessible by boat.'

Once through the gates, they drove for a couple of minutes before reaching the main house, strategically situated among a few pine trees to ensure the building wasn't visible from either the lake or the main city centre.

Suzannah got out and stretched her legs and looked at the main house, which wasn't so much a house as a castle and then looked out over the lake at the fabulous view ahead.

'Funny, I can look down and see the lake and the town from here, but I don't remember seeing the castle from the lakeside, but its quite a size, I'd have thought I'd have noticed it from the town,' said Suzannah.

'Clever isn't it. Mr Di Stefano put in a lot of thought to putting these strategically-placed trees to obscure the view from anyone below us, but to allow him to look over the whole of Lugano below. You see there's a forest behind the estate and from the town or the lakeside, the few trees around the house just look like part of the forest,' said Dante with some pride.

'Ingenious,' agreed Suzannah.

'Have you eaten yet? The grounds here are quite extensive and if I show you everything, we will be walking for several hours. And Mr Di Stefano sent word to make sure you were well looked after today.'

'That's very kind of him. I must admit I rushed out without breakfast.'

'Ah, come in and have a coffee and brioche before we start.'

Dante lead her into a room, near to the front entrance of the castle, which was the main dining-room and had a wonderful view of the lake. The décor was very modern — large solid pieces of dark furniture, contrasted strongly with the stark white walls. Somehow this surprised Suzannah, although she hadn't given it any thought, she had assumed the place would be stuffed with antiques and paintings, not minimalist.

Suzannah looked out and watched the tourist boats on the lake, while Dante made coffee and warmed up the pastries.

'Here we are,' said Dante, as he came in with a tray. 'The ones on the left are marmalade and those on the right are chocolate.

'Thank you. Are you not having any?'

'I ate earlier, but please help yourself.' Suzannah did so and took a bite. The pastries were very fresh, baked only a couple of hours ago and the exquisite taste aroused her hunger and she ate two.

While she finished her coffee, Suzannah realised she hadn't heard any sounds in the house from other staff and thought this a little odd, but she knew that Mr Di Stefano was known to be an extremely private man and guessed that keeping staffing to a minimum probably helped maintain his privacy.

'Tell me, Dante, are you as interested in art and plants as Mr Di Stefano?'

Dante smiled, 'Actually yes. That's how I ended up working for him. I trained as a lawyer, but took a sabbatical to do some conservation work in Indonesia and met Mr Di Stefano there.'

'What kind of conservation work?'

'Orchids are no different to other rare and endangered species of either plants or animals. Their habitat is often under threat from deforestation, where trees on the edges of jungle forests are cut down, for charcoal, for example. As a consequence there is literally less room for the indigenous plants and animals. This is a particular problem if those specimens have a fascination for humans, like orchids or indeed tigers.'

'Rich men covet them so the poorer local population give them the orchids, further jeopardising their long term future,' said Suzannah.

'Exactly,' said Dante. 'You really do understand.'

Suzannah thought he seemed surprised and could tell that even under his carefully controlled exterior, this was a subject Dante cared for passionately.

'Mr Di Stefano isn't someone who collects plants, just for his pleasure, if he takes specimens away, he also takes away soil samples and sponsors a lot of work into understanding the best environments for the continued survival of these plants in the wild and also tries to look at ways the local economies can be improved . . . '

' . . . to prevent the need for the poorer communities to further degrade the forest to make ends meet.'

'Yes, exactly. Mr Di Stefano doesn't advertise this aspect of his life, as it is a subject close to his heart and I would appreciate your discretion with this.'

'Of course, Dante. Does he go to these remote places himself?'

'Yes. That's partly why we don't

advertise the fact. Some of these plants come from very unstable countries. If it was known that someone as rich as Mr Di Stefano came in person, the risk of kidnap would be very strong indeed. We have ways of minimising his risk, but even so.'

Suzannah thought a moment in silence.

'You look deep in thought,' said Dante.

'Me, oh sorry, I was just imagining you and Mr Di Stefano ploughing through remote jungle rescuing plants, dodging kidnappers.'

'Like Indiana Jones?' said Dante.

'Yes, just like Indiana Jones!' This was the first time Suzannah had seen Dante laugh — his face was transformed and for the first time Suzannah realised how handsome he was.

At once, his face darkened, as if he'd caught himself relaxing a moment and his mask returned.

'Right, well if you've had enough to eat, let me show you the grounds,' said

Dante, formally.

'Good,' replied Suzannah, as she stood up.

Why is he being so formal? I'll be gone tomorrow; he'll never see me again. And his boss is away. He seems to want to hide behind his mask, thought Suzannah and intuitively realised that he was a man with many dark secrets.

The grounds were indeed more extensive than Suzannah imagined, extending steeply down the mountainside from the pine forest behind to the shores of the lake below. Looking up to the top of the mountain, beyond the forest, it seemed densely covered in vegetation with no housing.

Beyond this peak, were other taller mountains, visible in the distance with snow-capped peaks.

Suzannah wondered why Mr Di Stefano had asked Dante to show her all the estate, but didn't like to ask. She was having fun, but was glad she had worn trousers and sturdy shoes, as most of the grounds were surprisingly unkempt and weed ridden.

'Sorry it's a bit of a mess. Our gardener . . . ' Dante hesitated a moment, 'left and we haven't replaced him yet. I take care of the greenhouses, but don't have time to sort out anything else. Ah, here are the greenhouses.' Dante held the door open for Suzannah to go in and closed it immediately behind them, to maintain the carefully controlled temperature inside.

Suzannah saw the thermostats and sectioning of areas according to whether the plants preferred more sunlight or shade.

The three greenhouses each had different, carefully controlled humidity levels, mimicking, as best they could the exact conditions of their origin. Attached to one greenhouse was a mini laboratory, for soil analysis.

Although walking round the grounds in the sunshine was wonderful in itself, on seeing the greenhouses, Suzannah was both astonished and overcome.

This was an oasis for rare plants she could only have ever dreamed of.

Orchids were special and were a plant that inspired passion in enthusiasts. Suzannah had such feelings and truly appreciated what she was seeing: an oasis for breeding rare and valuable plants.

Suzannah crouched down by a bloom admiring the colouring of brown freckles on the cream background of the plant.

'Are you all right, Suzannah?' said Dante.

'Oh I'm sorry, I'm just a bit awestruck I think. This looks like a phalaenopsis gigantean, I've never seen one before, only photographs in books.'

'Correct. I'm impressed. We picked it up in Borneo and have been quite successful in cultivating it.

'It's so beautiful. They're all so beautiful. I love how you haven't arranged all this like a rich man's gallery. You really are trying to learn about these aren't you. Not just collect them for the sake of it.'

'Mr Di Stefano has many contacts with brilliant, and indeed discreet, botanists from some of the world's top universities. We couldn't do it without outside help and in turn Mr Di Stefano sponsors a lot of research and conservation projects.'

'I hope you don't mind me asking, but all I know about Mr Di Stefano is that he's a businessman, but I don't exactly know what kind of business he's in,' said Suzannah. She hoped the question didn't seem as if she was prying too much. To her relief, Dante answered her without hesitation.

'Mr Di Stefano comes from a wealthy banking family. He has a background in banking and law and originally was going to continue the family business, but you could say he is a bit of an entrepreneur and rather excelled at judging which markets were up and coming and made a lot of money on the stock exchange. With this money he funds his conservation work and also builds his well-known sculpture collection.'

'An amazing man, I think,' said Suzannah. Dante nodded.

* * *

When they finished the tour of greenhouses, Dante led Suzannah outside and continued the tour; after which, he made her a coffee and by this time, Dante at last seemed more relaxed and Suzannah enjoyed talking to him, the strain of their first encounter having been completely dispelled.

'By the way, I'm sorry about the other night, when I asked about your friend. It was rude of me and no, Mr Di Stefano didn't ask me to apologise to you.'

'It's all right, he explained you had to be watchful and blunt as part of your job. I've known Mac for years. We were at art school together and he's like a brother to me. I think his work's fantastic, he deserves to have a good career.'

Dante nodded and was about to speak when the phone rang. It felt like an intrusion and Suzannah noticed Dante's expression immediately harden. The call was clearly something serious and when Dante finally hung up, he looked like he was searching for the right words.

'You don't need to explain,' said Suzannah. 'I can tell that was an important call and I really must be going anyway, but thank you so much for the tour, Dante. And do thank Mr Di Stefano for me and tell him that as soon as I get back to the UK, I'm going to do some more work in clay and I'll send you some photographs of what I produce.'

'When do you go return to England?' asked Dante.

'Tomorrow afternoon,' replied Suzannah.

Did I imagine that he looked disappointed when I said that? she wondered to herself.

3

Suzannah spent the rest of the day looking out over the water, as the shadows lengthened in the sunshine and thought about how lovely Lugano was and also about her extraordinary day. Suzannah also gradually began to wonder if it was only the plants that had overwhelmed her so much during her visit to Mr Di Stefano's estate. Dante? No, surely not. And she dispelled the unsettling thought from her mind.

Later on, Suzannah and Mac were meeting up to go out for dinner, but for now, Suzannah was glad to be alone, she needed to think. She got up from the bench and went over to a snack stall and bought a panini, but after one bite, realised she wasn't really hungry and broke up the bread and fed it to a swiftly-gathering crowd of ducks, sparrows and even a swan. The bread was soon gone and with a smile, Suzannah watched the birds finish their meal and strolled by the lakeside back towards her hotel.

When she got back, someone at the main desk was having a heated discussion with one of the guests and the receptionist therefore forgot to give Suzannah her message when he gave her the key.

'I want to change rooms at once. We were promised a view of the lake.'

'I'm sorry, sir . . . '

Suzannah hurried to her room, the sound of the unhappy guest's raised voice had somehow broken the spell of her peaceful mind. And quite suddenly the whole day seemed like a dream. Impossibly wonderful and too good to be true.

'Come in,' said Suzannah, sadly, on hearing a knock at the door.

'Come in?' said Mac. 'I thought you were supposed to say Avanti.'

'Yes, but I knew it was you.'

'You did? Oh well. Anyway are you ready to go out, I'm starving. Oh and I'm paying. Mrs Baxter didn't just buy all my stuff, she is a very nice lady and paid up promptly so . . . '

'Great. We can go to a five star restaurant then,' teased Suzannah.

'Well, I know that check I've just paid in has cleared my overdraft but . . . '

'I'm only kidding, Mac. I know you've got debts. Look, I passed somewhere near the south shore of the lake earlier. It looked nice and wasn't too expensive.'

'Sounds good. You know it was really smart of you to keep your horticulture thing going. I wish I'd learnt to do something other than art. It would prevent many sleepless nights.'

'Don't worry about it, Mac. No point in looking back and besides, I really think your career is going to take off now. Mrs Baxter isn't a one off, I overheard a lot of conversations on our preview night and your work created a buzz.'

'Really?'

'Really. I know a lot of people liked your work and it outshone the rest of us by a long way. I really think you should explore doing more business over here. Switzerland has a good tradition of nurturing the arts and your work has I think caught the zeitgeist.'

Mac blushed. 'You think so?'

'I know so. Here.' Suzannah tossed a newspaper to Mac, which was folded back to the arts pages. A reporter had been to the preview night and gave a brief description of the British work on show.

'Have you got to the bit, which talks about the exciting work of newcomer Mark MacKenzie yet?' said Suzannah with a smile. Mac scanned the page in disbelief, and then reread it, just to make sure.

'I can't believe it! Can I keep this?'

'Of course you can. Nothing of my work, or anyone else's was even mentioned. Mac you are the star of the show. Anyway, shall we go, I'm starving.

And I think we need to do a bit of celebrating on our last night here in Lugano, don't you?' Mac smiled.

'Ok, I agree. Hey hang on, didn't you go up to Mr big-shot's place today? How'd you get on?'

Suzannah told Mac about her wonderful day, as vaguely as she could. She didn't want to break any confidences. As they reached the lobby, the troublesome new arrival was still there, and was still unhappy. Now the manager had got involved and was trying to sort things out.

'I'm sorry, sir, but all our lakeside rooms are taken.' In the ensuing tension, Suzannah slipped her key to the red-faced receptionist, who was once again too preoccupied to give Suzannah her waiting message.

The restaurant Suzannah chose was perfect. Over dinner, she and Mac watched the sun set over the lake and the last of the tourist boats return, as darkness fell. And the baked trout was fantastic.

Unusually, Mac and Suzannah didn't find much to talk about, both were preoccupied with their own thoughts and were a little sad about it being their last night in such a wonderful place.

After dinner, Mac suggested they do a tour of the bars and sample some of the nightlife, but Suzannah was tired and wanted an early night. She also wanted to be alone with her thoughts.

On the walk back to the hotel, Suzannah sensed a change in Mac's mood, he was clearly deep in thought and something was troubling him.

'Penny for them?' said Suzannah at last.

'Oh it's nothing. Really,' replied Mac. Suzannah wasn't convinced, but didn't pry further.

★   ★   ★

When they reached the entrance of the hotel, Suzannah started to climb the entrance steps, but Mac tugged at her sleeve.

'Wait a minute. Can we talk out here for a moment? I'll lose my nerve once we're inside.'

'Sure,' said Suzannah, 'I thought something was on your mind.'

'It's not something: it's someone. You.' Mac pulled Suzannah towards him and kissed her.

Suzannah hadn't anticipated her old friend had such feelings for her and felt confused and after a moment pulled away. 'I'm sorry, Mac. I had no idea . . . '

'You don't need to apologise, I do. I'm sorry, Suzannah. I just wanted to be more than just good friends, but your kiss has told me otherwise.' Mac darted up the steps and didn't turn round when Suzannah called his name.

'Suzannah.' Suzannah spun round to see Dante standing behind her and wondered how long he'd been there.

'Dante!'

'Didn't you get my message?'

'What message?' said Suzannah.

'I've been in touch with Mr Di Stefano since you left. I must admit Mr Di Stefano invited you today, not just to show you round, but for me to give you an informal interview. He'd like to offer you a job, looking after the grounds. There's an old shed on the estate that Mr Di Stefano says you can have as a studio for your work.

'He doesn't want you to give up on that, but as I'm sure you can imagine, even among gardeners, not many have the inclination to look after rare orchids.' Suzannah was too stunned to say anything for a moment.

'I'm sorry. I can tell this is a bad time. But I've been instructed to give you the message before you fly back to England tomorrow. If you want to sleep on it, I don't need a decision tonight, but Mr Di Stefano is someone who likes to get things sorted quickly and I'll need a decision first thing in the morning, before you leave. If you want the job, ring me in the morning and don't catch your plane. I'll sort out your visa requirements. I just need to know.'

Suzannah thought a moment, trying to take everything in. 'Dante, I'm stunned, I really am. I didn't expect this at all.'

'I know. That was the intention. At the gallery, Mr Di Stefano took an instant liking to you and your combined interests, as well as your superb Italian made Mr Di Stefano want to hire you on the spot. But I needed to make some enquiries first. Sorry, we check out any potential employee to make sure their background is what they say it is. Yours checks out.'

Suzannah's head began to clear and although she listened carefully to Dante, she couldn't help notice the warmth she felt in his company earlier that day had vanished and was replaced with the brusque coolness she first noticed in the man. It was nothing she could specifically pinpoint, just that the mask had come down.

I wonder if he saw Mac kiss me and

43

thinks I'm a liar and that we're an item,
she thought to herself.

'Anyway, I'll leave you now to think
things over,' said Dante.

'You don't need to, I've already
decided,' replied Suzannah. 'I'll take the
job. I've no ties in the UK and as
you've probably found out from your
private investigator, I've no family alive,
so, there is no one I need to consult
with and I've no reason to turn down
such a generous offer. Besides I really
want the job. I love it here in Lugano.'

★   ★   ★

Suzannah moved into her room at the
castle, the day she started working for
Mr Di Stefano, which was exactly one
week after Dante first offered it to her.
The room was offered rent free, until
Suzannah found suitable accommodation in the city.

There was a lot to sort out, arranging
her stuff to be brought over from
England and not having to look for

44

accommodation immediately gave Suzannah a chance to sort out her affairs in the UK.

The park, where she worked part time were understanding about her leaving so quickly and agreed that she couldn't have turned down such an offer and would forward on her pay-cheque.

A company recommended by Dante took care of packing up Suzannah's stuff, *(overseen by Mac, who was now back in the UK)*, and put it into storage, ready to be delivered to Switzerland, once she had found a place of her own. As Suzannah had been living in rented accommodation, it wasn't too difficult to sort out, although her landlord kept her deposit because of the short notice given.

Mac helped as much as he could and Suzannah was relieved that they were still friends. Although she loved Mac dearly, it was only in a platonic way and he had been very understanding about it when they finally talked things over.

On her first day at work, one of the first things Dante did was give Suzannah a large file to study. It contained strict instructions, to be followed to the letter, on how to care for the orchids in the greenhouses, as well as codes for the alarms on the house and the greenhouses. The rest of the grounds were left to her discretion as to how to tidy them up, although she had been told not to chop down any trees.

Apart from herself and Dante, there was only one other member of staff, a housekeeper, Angela: a local woman of perhaps fifty years of age, who came in daily to take care of the house.

From talking to her, Suzannah gathered that the reason Mr Di Stefano seemed to have so few staff here was that he was rarely there.

When he wasn't away on business, he was in remote areas of the globe pursuing his conservation work. Without it being specifically mentioned, Suzannah also guessed that it was Mr Di Stefano's desire for privacy that kept the number of staff at his home at a minimum.

During those first few days at the Di Stefano estate, Suzannah's first priority was to learn exactly how to care for the orchids. Dante went through the protocols with her and watching him tend the plants with such care and attention to detail, Suzannah realised that this was a real passion for him; feelings he couldn't conceal.

As Dante was going to be away the following week, Suzannah wanted to make sure she was fully familiar with the particular needs of the exotic plants before he went. Suzannah knew Dante and Mr Di Stefano were putting a lot of trust in her abilities by leaving many delicate, valuable and much-loved blooms in her care.

As the day of Dante's departure approached, Suzannah was a little disappointed that since she had been working with him, Dante had been generally aloof. She had hoped to see more of the Dante she met that wonderful afternoon on the estate, but instead, he wasn't so much cool as cold, bordering on rude at times.

Suzannah didn't know why and hoped he was just preoccupied with his forthcoming trip and tried not to take it personally.

She sensed something was on his mind and for some reason she couldn't explain, she wanted to help. Also, Suzannah knew that if her job was to be a success, she and Dante had to get along. She would rarely see Mr Di Stefano and if Dante didn't like her, Suzannah realised she wouldn't be in Lugano for long.

Suzannah generally liked to get up early, at around six-thirty and on the day Dante was due to leave on business, Suzannah hoped, on rising, to catch him before he left, to wish him a good trip and was a little disappointed to discover later on, from Angela that he had left around five thirty in the morning.

Although there was no reason for it,

Suzannah felt a little sad. On reflection, she wondered if Dante's general formality was just a cultural difference between them and hoped he would be a little friendlier once he got to know her.

Trying not to dwell on things, Suzannah grabbed a coffee and brioche, which Angela ordered in for her and went straight to the orchid greenhouses to water the plants. It hadn't taken Suzannah long to get to grips with their needs, her file was very clear and left nothing to chance. As such, she had plenty of time to think about not only future art projects, but how best to manage the grounds of the rest of the estate.

The steep incline of the land did pose some problems. Around the greenhouses a large terrace had been made to accommodate them within an artificially flattened area, but the rest of the estate was on an incline.

In the northeast area, between the greenhouse terrace and the perimeter fence, bordering the forest, Suzannah had in mind to build an alpine rockery.

She thought it would be a good way of making a favourable impression with Dante if she had a large amount of it accomplished before he returned. With Mr Di Stefano being away so much, Dante was effectively her boss and Suzannah determined to make a positive impact with her work.

Suzannah was used to hard physical work, not only because of her previous work with the National park, but also metalwork had developed her strength. Being tall, this work hadn't bulked up her figure and people were often surprised how someone so seemingly willowy could do so much.

★　★　★

The rockery didn't take long to plan. She'd already had experience of building a large one before, and Suzannah soon established that Mr Di Stefano had a well-equipped tool shed and with Angela's help, they located somewhere that stocked suitable rocks and plants. All that needed to be done was for the land to be cleared.

'Are you sure about all this,' said Angela nervously, after hearing what Suzannah was going to do.

'Why not? It looks a mess and Dante said I have a completely free hand, not including the greenhouses, obviously. Don't you think a rockery will brighten up that area?'

'I suppose it will,' conceded Angela.

'Another thing, all that shrubbery is taking quite a bit of light from the greenhouse, the bushes are far too overgrown. It will be hard work, but once I'm done, the greenhouses will have much more light, which I think will suit them.'

'I'm beginning to see what you mean. It's a good idea, Suzannah. I doubt anyone would have thought of it. I think you're just what this old place needed, you know.'

Suzannah made sketches of the northeast area of the estate, where she had in mind to put the alpine rockery and her ideas rapidly took shape. The more Suzannah thought about it, the better the idea seemed.

To clear the area of overgrown shrubbery, Suzannah hired some power tools, then dug through the soil. This took a full four long days of heavy labour.

Suzannah started work at six-thirty and only finished around nightfall. The only break Suzannah took during the day, was when Angela came out and insisted she come inside for some lunch, which she gobbled down before rushing back outside.

When the soil was fully prepared, Suzannah had the rocks delivered and she managed to get them in place, forming irregular tiers ready for planting. Suzannah didn't put the stones in too neatly, she wanted the whole area to look as natural as possible.

Suzannah even considered including a water feature, cascading down the rocks, but after thinking this over, she thought she'd leave it for now and perhaps include this at a later date, as there was just one day remaining for planting before Dante was due to return and she wanted it to look complete, to surprise him.

After working an eighteen-hour day, the rockery was finally finished and Suzannah was exhausted, covered in soil from all the planting, but happy and looking forward to Dante's return and seeing his expression on seeing all her hard work.

4

After packing her suitcase, Suzannah sat on her bed and tried not to cry, but the feeling was overwhelming and eventually gave way to her tears, she was bitterly disappointed at Dante's reaction to the rockery and had never considered he would be anything other than happy with her work. Suzannah sobbed into her pillow until exhaustion took over and she fell asleep.

When she woke up it was dark and Suzannah looked at the clock — 8 p.m. 'I've been asleep forever! That will be something else Dante will be cross about.' Suzannah went to the window to close the curtains and noticed Dante's car wasn't parked outside and she hoped he wasn't in.

Suzannah realised he could return at any minute, because as well as being his place of work, this estate was also his home. Suzannah wanted to be out of there before he got back.

Thinking fast, she planned to go downstairs and phone her old hotel from the hall, book a room and ask them to send a cab for her and her things. Suzannah knew she should leave a note, but thought she would fax it from the hotel. At that moment, she didn't want to stay at the Di Stefano estate a moment longer.

Suzannah opened her door quietly and listened. Silence. As she shut her door, she noticed an envelope pinned to the back of it. She recognised the handwriting immediately, it was from Dante. Who else.

Dear Suzannah,

Angela's made you some soup and there's a bottle of wine on the table, please help yourself. I've gone into town — I've some things to sort out and I won't be back until tomorrow, so you will have the place to yourself overnight. I've done what needs doing in the greenhouses, so the orchids won't need any attention until morning.

The more I think things through, the more I wonder if you were right after all. The north side of the estate is vulnerable, I suppose we've thought all that shrubbery gave us some protection, but you were correct, it doesn't.

I really am sorry to have upset you. I overreacted. Anyway, I hope you are feeling better. Angela told me about the long hours you've been putting in on the rockery and it does look good.

Just one thing. Please would you make sure you stay in the house overnight. You know how the burglar alarm works and I would appreciate it from a security point of view. We do need to tighten up security here. I have you to thank for drawing my attention to that. Until we do, I don't want to leave the place untended.

If you have any problems, call my

mobile or the police. Do not, repeat do not go outside if you suspect any intruders on the premises. Set off the emergency button, situated under my desk in the study and wait for the police.

This button is linked to the police station and help will arrive shortly after it is activated. There's a gun in my desk drawer if you need it, but I don't anticipate any problems.

Regards
Dante.

Suzannah reread the letter as she warmed up the soup and thought through her options. When the delicious squash soup was piping hot, she ate it in the kitchen and then had a second helping. Angela didn't usually prepare anything for her evening meal and Suzannah was thankful for her kindness. She must have realised I was very upset.

By now, Suzannah felt a lot better and had come to the conclusion that it would probably still be best if she leave. She was used to being independent and although she was grateful for Dante's apology, she knew that a fiery working relationship between two people was untenable.

Clearly Dante liked things done a certain way. His way. Suzannah was a challenge to that. Reluctantly, she decided to stay overnight, for Mr Di Stefano's sake as much as anything.

Suzannah looked at Dante's letter again, as she poured herself a glass of wine. Mr Di Stefano's hardly ever here, yet this place has an emergency button connected to the police station. I wonder . . .

Suzannah picked up her wine glass and went into Dante's study and found the panic button and the gun. Suzannah put her hand out to touch the weapon, but withdrew it nervously; she had never touched such a weapon before and certainly didn't know how to use it.

Sitting at Dante's desk, Suzannah

sipped her wine and thought it likely that Mr Di Stefano's world famous sculpture collection might indeed be within these castle walls. But if so, why no guard dogs? Or CCTV cameras? Suzannah thought she knew why.

She guessed that the visible presence of state of the art security would actually draw attention to the estate and she guessed that the artwork must be in a remote, but hidden section of the castle. But where?

Curiosity suddenly gripped Suzannah and she decided to see if she could have a look at Mr Di Stefano's collection of sculptures. After all, she assumed this would be her last night in Mr Di Stefano's employ and it would probably be her only chance.

The idea both frightened her and thrilled her. Although she only wanted to have a peek at the collection, she hadn't been given permission to do so and she knew she really shouldn't. Oh why not. I'm not going to even touch anything — I just want to have a look.

Pouring out a second glass of wine, Suzannah looked up with a start on hearing thunder. She went over to the window and saw the lashing rain against the pane. The storm had started suddenly and violently.

Ordinarily, Suzannah would have stayed by the window to watch the lightning over the lake. Now she was distracted and tried to think where the sculptures could be.

She had already seen all the rooms on the ground floor and she immediately discounted this area. Her own room was on the first floor. Although she didn't know what was in the other rooms of the first floor, she guessed that Mr Di Stefano wouldn't put his prized collection anywhere near the guest rooms.

The second and third floors housed Dante's room and Mr Di Stefano's private quarters. Suzannah had never been higher than the first floor and decided against prying into such a private area. If the sculptures were there, she would just have to miss seeing them.

Suzannah walked over to the window to watch the storm, already discounting her idea of searching for the art collection as a stupid idea. However, her mind still considered it and she realised that the castle had an old bell tower and she wondered if this remote area of the castle might be the location of the artwork.

The other possibility was if the place had a cellar. Although Suzannah had never noticed one, it seemed impossible for a castle not to have one.

Bell tower or cellar? Suzannah decided to try the bell tower first, if nothing else, the view of the storm from there would be spectacular. Suzannah searched the west wing of the ground floor looking for the stairway that would lead to the bell tower.

Suzannah had visited enough castles before to guess that the spiral stairway she was looking for would most likely begin on the ground floor.

Suzannah went into the study and felt along the walls, but couldn't find any hidden entrances and was about to go into the kitchen when she noticed the edge of the large rug was folded under and went to flatten it, to stop anyone tripping on it, when she instinctively lifted it up.

'Bingo!' The wooden floor revealed a trap door and Suzannah had a hunch the Mr Di Stefano's famous art collection was beneath it. After all, the location of the emergency button and gun fitted in. Dante spent most of his time in that study, which functioned as his office, he was also the Di Stefano collection's armed guard.

Suzannah was at once convinced she was right and she lifted up the trap door and looked below. It was too dark to see clearly, but Suzannah remembered seeing a torch in the study drawer, alongside the handgun and she went back for it before descending the cellar steps.

She could feel her heart thumping

and although nervous, was still too excited to turn back.

Once at the bottom of the steps, Suzannah found a light switch and saw that there in front of her was a wine cellar. Stopping to look at the bottles, Suzannah guessed that this was no ordinary wine cellar — none of the labels looked familiar and Suzannah assumed that these were rare and valuable vintages.

Feeling a little calmer, Suzannah took a deep breath and looked round, searching each wall in turn, but couldn't see any of the sculptures. All seemed in order, the only thing that surprised Suzannah was the relatively small size of the cellar. She somehow thought it would be bigger.

Thinking she had nothing else to discover, Suzannah turned back towards the steps and switched off the light. For no particular reason, Suzannah kept her hand on the light-switch and to her surprise, the prolonged push she gave it caused the wine rack to move away revealing a steel doorway, with a coded push button entry.

It looked like a large safe and she knew there was no way she would be able to pass through it, but she smiled to herself on finding the probable location of the Di Stefano art collection and gently touched the door before retracing her steps, trying to replace everything as she went so no one would know she had been down in the cellar. The same movement on the light-switch returned the wine rack to its original location and Suzannah returned to the study.

Once back on ground level, Suzannah picked up her discarded glass of wine and went into the kitchen to wash up. By now, she felt more than a little guilty at snooping round and was almost glad she couldn't get beyond the steel door.

While she dried the pots, Suzannah looked round the kitchen, to see if there was anything else that needed washing up, when she suddenly noticed a door.

'Of course!' Suzannah put down the tea-towel and opened the door and found the stairwell to the bell tower. This door wasn't in any way concealed and was so obvious, Suzannah hadn't even registered its presence before now. As the storm was still raging, Suzannah climbed the steps, eagerly anticipating the fabulous view of the lake when she reached the top.

Although used to exercise, the winding steps were steep and by the time she reached the top, Suzannah felt a little dizzy. The view from the top though was amazing.

In the daylight, the whole estate would be clearly visible. Now, Suzannah looked down at the city lights and across the lake, which was periodically lit with lightning. Wow! This view is stunning.

As she watched the lake, Suzannah promised herself that she would return at first light and see the wonderful vista by day. It would be her final farewell to Lugano.

She intended to leave the estate immediately afterwards, hoping she would be able to leave before Dante returned. She knew it would be harder to say goodbye if she saw him face to face.

Suzannah took a deep breath in the crisp, sharp air and the last of the residual turmoil left her. This job was worth a try, but it didn't work out. Dante. Just as her thoughts returned to Dante, Suzannah caught sight of something from the corner of her eye. She looked towards the north region of the estate and saw a flash of light again.

It was a torch beam. The north side of the estate bordered only forest, there were no houses and at this time of night, Suzannah realised there was a strong possibility that thieves were trying to enter the estate.

Suzannah waited, involuntarily holding her breath. She saw it again. This time the beam came from inside the estate. They had climbed over the perimeter fence and were now on the estate.

Realising there was no time to waste, Suzannah raced down the spiral staircase, as fast as she could. By the time she reached the kitchen, she was breathless. First she checked the burglar alarm was activated, if anyone tried to break a window, the alarm would go off. The greenhouses were similarly alarmed. Next, Suzannah dashed into the study and got the gun,

Picking up the phone, Suzannah was about to phone the police, when she hesitated. The approach from the road took a long time and any intruders would have plenty of time to escape as soon as they heard the sirens.

Suzannah thought the intruders would want to steal either the orchids or the sculptures, whichever it was, she'd know soon enough. Alternatively, they could be on a scouting exercise, sizing the place up, in which case, Suzannah thought it would be better to catch them.

Something nagged at Suzannah. She felt guilty that her work clearing the shrubbery had made any would-be thieves task easier and she felt a responsibility to catch them.

This way she felt she could make up for her oversight. Suzannah picked up the gun and felt the weight in her hand.

Next she picked up the torch, but put it straight back down. She intended to creep up on the intruders and if she used a flashlight, it might alert them to her presence.

Suzannah had good night vision and she felt she knew every shrub and every inch of the estate and would therefore be better off without a torch.

Suzannah crept out of the back door, reset the alarm and waited. The only sounds she could hear were from the rain and thunder. Walking quickly, but as quietly as possible, Suzannah headed north, towards where she saw the flashlights from the bell tower and after a couple of minutes heard hushed voices.

As she was near the greenhouses, she

dashed behind one of them. It was a safe place. If she was threatened, all she had to do was break a pane of glass and the alarm would go off alerting the police.

After a few seconds, her ears adjusted and she was able to establish that there were two men and could pick up snatches of conversation.

'How will you silence the girl?'

Suzannah put her hand to her mouth to stop herself screaming. The man asking the question had a familiar voice, although he was whispering and the sound of the rain muffled his voice, his identity suddenly flooded Suzannah's mind.

Dante!

5

Straining to hear against the lashing wind, Suzannah couldn't pick out every word that was spoken, but she deduced that Dante was briefing this person about the layout of the estate.

She also heard names of famous sculptures, probably those in Mr Di Stefano's collection. Before long, Suzannah was fairly sure they were planning something for the future and not this night. Tonight was a trial run, for reconnaissance.

Suzannah's first instinct was to confront them with the gun, but she knew Dante knew how to use such a weapon; she didn't, he probably knew that. In a confrontation, she would soon be overwhelmed.

Instead, Suzannah crept back to the house, reset the alarm, replaced the gun and went upstairs to her room to change into dry clothes and to think. Of one thing she was sure; whatever happened now, she planned to stay and foil Dante's plan to steal the sculptures. She owed Mr Di Stefano that much.

She also knew that even if she managed to contact Mr Di Stefano and tell him all she knew, he might not believe her and quite probably, Dante would then be wise as to what she had learned. I'll just have to stay here, try not to get fired and keep watch, thought Suzannah.

Just then, her thoughts were interrupted by a soft knocking at her door. Damn!

'Hello?' said Suzannah cautiously, making no attempt to open the door.

'Sorry, to bother you,' said Dante. 'I saw your light was on when I came in and thought we should talk, if you're feeling up to it.'

'I'm getting changed, I'll meet you in the kitchen in ten minutes,' said Suzannah.

'OK,' said Dante.

Suzannah had been so wrapped up in her thoughts, she hadn't heard Dante come in and she had ten minutes to think of an excuse as to why she had been out in the rain. Her long hair was still wet and she guessed Dante must have seen her footprints downstairs.

'Hi, I've made some tea and put a splash of brandy in it,' said Dante.

'Thanks,' said Suzannah with a smile. She had no intention of letting him have any inkling of her thoughts.

'I finished up my business early and to be honest, I hoped I'd be able to see you tonight. I had a bad feeling you might have left if I didn't.'

'I certainly thought about it, but actually you were right. I should have considered the security of the estate. I made a mistake.'

Dante looked at her quizzically. 'Been out? It's a horrible night.'

'You think so? I love storms. I went outside to look at the lightening over the lake. I've never seen anything like it

72

before. I didn't stray far from the door-way.'

'Ah, you're not afraid of thunder, then.'

'Not at all.'

The silence between them throbbed with unspoken thoughts. Suzannah looked into her tea and took a sip; she could sense questions brooding in Dante's mind.

'You know, I really am glad you decided to stay. I'd feel very sad if you left because I'd scared you off. And I would have had a lot of explaining to do when I next spoke to Mr Di Stefano, if you left like that.' Dante looked at Suzannah, she could feel the burning intensity of his eyes, but she couldn't look at him directly and kept her gaze on her tea.

'I went back and had another look at the rockery and you've really done a fine job.'

'Thank you,' said Suzannah simply.

'Over the next couple of weeks I will be updating the security for the estate.

You were quite right, a child could scale that perimeter fence. I'm looking into improvements.'

'Do you want me to help?' said Suzannah, looking at him for the first time. Dante was clearly surprised at this and for a moment the shock was clearly visible, before the familiar, expressionless mask returned.

'Thanks, I'll let you know.'

Suzannah burned to know why Dante seemed to want her to stay. If he's planning to rob Mr Di Stefano, surely he'd want me out of the way. Unless . . . unless he needs a scapegoat!

'Are you all right?' said Dante.

'Oh sorry, I was miles away. Look I'm sorry, I'm really tired and it's getting late.'

'Of course. Now I'm back, why don't you have a lie in, you look exhausted. I can water the plants in the morning.'

'No, I'd like to do it, if that's all right. I liked getting up early and it will give me time to think of how to tidy up the rest of the estate. If you don't mind.'

'Suzannah. I love what you've done already and please, do whatever you want with the rest, just don't chop down any trees.'

'Don't worry, I wouldn't have done anyway. Now I think I'll go to bed.'

Suzannah got up, smiled at Dante and turned to leave the kitchen.

'Suzannah?'

'Yes,' said Suzannah turning round again. Dante wanted to say something.

'It's nothing. Goodnight. Sleep well.'

Once back in her room, Suzannah slid the bolt and sighed. Keeping control in Dante's presence had been hard. Now, the adrenaline made Suzannah at once nauseous and shivery.

Her hands and feet felt cold and clammy, yet her forehead was hot. Suzannah sat down on the bed and took some deep breaths.

Get a grip, she told herself. Gradually the sickness subsided and she wrapped a blanket round her shoulders, which lessened the shivering.

After a few minutes her racing

thoughts subsided and Suzannah began to feel better. Much better. In many ways, she reasoned that she had gone through the hardest part: dealing with Dante when she was still shocked at learning of his treachery.

Anything she learnt from now on, wouldn't be a surprise and she would be fully prepared. I'll trap you like a cat catching a mouse, Dante Candurro.

Now anger surged in her cheeks, as Suzannah thought of how Dante had betrayed Mr Di Stefano, someone who obviously trusted him implicitly. Also, Suzannah knew Mr Di Stefano frequently loaned out his art collection, he wasn't the kind of art collector who had his treasures hidden away, never letting the wider world see them.

Art thieves usually stole to order and Suzannah knew that Dante already would have a buyer in mind and once whisked away, the unique Di Stefano collection would never see the light of day again and be lost to the world.

Suzannah's resolve returned and she

had a hot shower, then flopped into bed and looked at the clock: 3.30 a.m. and fell quickly into an exhausted sleep.

Despite the turmoil of the previous evening, Suzannah woke up with her alarm and was instantly wide-awake. Dressing quickly, she went straight out to the greenhouses and watered the plants.

The morning was bright and crisp and the ground still soft from the previous evening.

When the orchids were tended, Suzannah locked up, set the alarm and looked out onto the sparkling crisp lake. The previous stormy and treacherous night seemed too improbable from the warm perspective of morning. With a shudder, Suzannah wished it had all been a dream, but she knew it was all too true.

Hiding her contempt in front of Dante would be her hardest challenge and Suzannah decided to think of him as little as possible to help her expression seem as neutral as possible.

Looking at the ground, Suzannah saw footprints from the previous evening. Three sets, one of which was clearly hers. She quickly checked no one was about, and then trampled over her own prints to obscure them. Now she looked towards where she had overheard the two conspirators talking last night and followed the prints.

One set, she presumed were Dante's, led back towards the house. The other set, slightly smaller than Dante's followed the perimeter fence and then stopped. Suzannah looked up, the six-foot wire fence and assumed the mystery person had scaled it.

'You look deep in thought.' Suzannah spun round to see Dante looking at her.

'Dante! You startled me,' said Suzannah, smiling.

'Sorry, I just came to see the orchids, but I see you've already done it.'

'Yes, no problems there, they all look healthy.'

Suzannah knew now that Dante had

seen her puzzling over the footprints and thought fast.

'You know, when I came up here, I was surprised to see some footprints. It looks as if someone might have been snooping round last night,' said Suzannah.

'You're very observant, but I wouldn't worry about it.' Suzannah was surprised at his reaction.

'You've already seen them, then?'

'Yes, probably just kids. But thanks for pointing it out. Have you made any plans for the south sector?'

'I can certainly work on that section next, if you like.'

'If you wouldn't mind. For anyone arriving by boat, the entrance doesn't give a great impression. When Mr Di Stefano visits, he often takes visitors on boat trips, so it might be the best place to smarten up.'

'No problem,' said Suzannah in a businesslike manner. 'I'll make some sketches after breakfast. Then I'll make a start clearing the road from the house to the southern entrance, it's very overgrown.

'Other than that, I'll think of some ideas, do more sketches, then let you see them before I start on anything.'

'There's no need, really.'

'No I'd prefer it. I don't want to repeat what happened last time. I think it's important for us to have a smooth professional working relationship, don't you?'

'Of course,' said Dante.

Suzannah sensed he wanted to say something else, but it seemed he thought better of it.

'I'll be very busy for the next few days, Suzannah. Please, I do trust your judgement. The rockery looks fabulous — do whatever you want with the land.'

'Fine,' said Suzannah. 'Oh, do you have any information on the soil here. I've a few ideas for plants, but I would need to know the results of a soil analysis.'

'One was done a few years ago, I'll see if we still have a record of it. If not, please get another one. As you know, we import earth for the orchids, no-one has ever bothered much with the soil out here before.'

'Hmm,' said Suzannah, thinking of what a waste. All this land, completely gone to seed.

'Why don't you let me cook you dinner tonight, as a peace offering.' This was the last thing Suzannah was expecting and could think of absolutely no reason to refuse.

'OK, that sounds nice,' said Suzannah finally.

'Anything you don't like to eat?' Suzannah shook her head.

'Good. Come downstairs about seven for an aperitif.'

6

For the rest of the morning, Suzannah made some sketches and walked round the south of the estate. This area was on an incline and the winding, single-track road that ran north to south, was partially obscured by overhanging, untended branches of trees and shrubs. Suzannah considered having the whole area terraced: a large undertaking that would need specialised vehicles and help to accomplish.

The thought of the forthcoming evening kept intruding into Suzannah's mind, distracting her from her task. Suzannah realised that Dante was being unusually nice and she wondered if he had an ulterior motive. Does he suspect I know of his thieving plans, I wonder?

Lunchtime came and went and Suzannah decided to work straight through, as much to avoid bumping into Dante, as much as anything. But by two thirty, Angela appeared, 'there you are! Hiding away, I've brought you some sandwiches and a drink.'

'You didn't need to, but thanks anyway.'

'Well to be honest, Dante put me up to it. I think he more worried about you wasting away than me, but don't tell him I said so.'

After Angela left, Suzannah sat down and ate her sandwiches, watching the sunlight twinkle on the lake. Dusting the crumbs from her lap, Suzannah stood up, stretched and started to clear any branches and debris that were lying across the road, thrown from neighbouring trees in the recent storm.

As the size of the area was large, it took most of the afternoon and by the time she had finished, she had a huge pile of wood.

Then, Suzannah sorted the pile and stripped off any foliage from the branches and chopped them into small pieces. When fully dried out, they would make extra logs for the living-room fire.

Suzannah had never seen this lit and realised that Mr Di Stefano's house, like the rest of his estate seemed to be in a permanently mothballed state. Always waiting for its patron to arrive and never truly lived in.

Suzannah intended to turn round the grounds, at the very least, before she left — to show Mr Di Stefano the previously unrealised potential of his fabulous estate. It's a shame I won't be here to enjoy it all, once I'm done. Suzannah fully intended to resign once she had trapped Dante. Somehow, she thought things would be very awkward for her, once his intention was publicly uncovered.

Dante was generally well liked and respected; she'd picked that up from talking to Angela, who clearly was a little in awe of him. Seems like I'm the only one who isn't, thought Suzannah, as she looked round for somewhere to put the wood to dry out. The skies were becoming overcast and Suzannah thought that it would probably rain soon.

'You've been busy,' said Dante.

'Oh, yes. I was just wondering where this lot could go to dry out. They'll make a wonderful log fire,' said Suzannah, a little wistfully.

'I think there's a canopy folded up somewhere in the garage. I'll go and find it.'

'I'll give you a hand,' said Suzannah. Before long, they erected a canopy, fixed against one side of the garage. It would shelter the wood while it dried out thoroughly. Suzannah expected Dante to leave her to stack the wood, but he pitched in and very soon everything was tidied away, just as they heard the first thunder roll rumbling in the distance.

'Come inside, or you'll get soaked. When it rains here it tends to be drenching.'

'So I've noticed,' said Suzannah looking up at the swirling navy-blue clouds.

They went inside and Dante offered to make some tea. Suzannah looked at the clock, it was already six o'clock.

'No thanks, I think I'll take a shower before dinner.'

'Yes, it's getting late. I'd better push on with cooking,' said Dante.

'What's for dinner,' asked Suzannah.

'You'll see,' said Dante. Suzannah couldn't help notice a twinkle flicker across his eyes, she sensed he wanted her to guess, but she decided not to play such games. By the smell, she could tell there was already a roast in the oven. It seemed wonderful, but she wasn't going to tell Dante that.

'OK, I'll be down in an hour,' said Suzannah simply and went upstairs.

While she showered, Suzannah heard a lot of crashes and several exclamations uttered from downstairs and she got the impression that cooking might not be one of Dante's strengths.

Suzannah dressed simply, changing into a casual wrap dress in teal cotton. After spending the day in jeans and a tee shirt, she wanted a change.

After giving her hair a brush, Suzannah put on some moisturiser. For makeup, she put on just a slick of mascara and lip gloss and went downstairs, determined to enjoy her meal, but not to let her guard down, even for a moment.

When she saw Dante, he looked flustered, but was clearly trying not to let it show.

'Aperitif?'

'Yes please,' said Suzannah.

'What would you like?'

'Something local. What do you recommend?'

'How about a bitter. They're very popular around here. The bitter taste isn't to everyone's liking and if you don't like it, don't be polite. But they do stimulate the appetite.'

'Sounds good, I'll give it a try.' Dante poured out two glasses of the bright red liquid. As she took a sip, Suzannah felt his attention upon her, watching for a response.

'Shall I pour you a glass of wine instead,' said Dante eventually.

'Was my expression that obvious?' said Suzannah. She thought she'd hidden the revulsion on tasting the liquid well.

'Not really, but many don't like it, so I was hedging my bets,' replied Dante passing her a glass of delicious sparkling prosecco.

'Ah, that's better. This is wonderful.'

'I know, it's grown over the Italian border, not too far from here.'

'As we're talking of wine ... ' Suzannah stopped when she heard a hissing sound coming from the kitchen.

'Damn!' said Dante. 'That'll be the soup. I'll be right back.'

After a few minutes of clattering, Dante returned, clutching two bowls of soup, looking as if they might bite.

'This smells wonderful, what is it?'

'Minestrone, but not any minestrone, it's an old family recipe.' Dante hesitated a moment before continuing. 'Well actually it's not from my family, it's an old recipe of Angela's, but I did make it myself.'

Suzannah picked up her spoon, here goes.

'It's delicious,' said Suzannah, a little surprised. And it was.

'Really?'

'Really,' said Suzannah who hungrily devoured it all a little too quickly to be polite.

Suzannah put down her bowl and noticed Dante was still only halfway through his.

'That was really delicious.'

'Good, would you like some more?' said Dante, standing up.

'I would, but please, stay where you are. I can find my way to the kitchen.'

'No,' he replied quickly. 'I insist. I'll get it, the kitchen isn't at its best right now. You stay right where you are.'

While Dante fetched a second helping of the delicious soup, Suzannah couldn't contain a smile, as she imagined the state of the kitchen. And of Angela's face when she saw it in the morning.

'Here we are,' said Dante, putting down the bowl in front of Suzannah.

'Thank you. This really is wonderful, you know, can I have the recipe?'

'I'll let you have a photocopy of mine.'

By the time Suzannah had finished her second bowl of soup, she felt much better, more relaxed and warmed all the way to her bones. The storm was nearly overhead now and on hearing a loud crash of thunder, Suzannah felt glad to be inside, glad to be here in Switzerland and to her surprise enjoying her dinner with Dante, far more than she ever expected.

'You really like storms, don't you?' said Dante.

'Yes, I do. I always feel a thrill of excitement when they approach. I particularly like it when I'm warm and snug inside, though.'

Dante smiled. 'I know what you

mean. Are you ready for your second course yet?'

'Absolutely,' said Suzannah.

While Dante returned to the kitchen to sort out the food, Suzannah went over to the window and watched the sheet and fork lightening over the lake and realised she was happy, happier than she had been in a long time, but then thoughts of Dante's treachery entered their mind like a storm cloud and her happiness was instantly dulled.

Several minutes later, Dante returned with two plates piled high with roast beef, roast potatoes, peas, carrots, Yorkshire pudding and onion gravy.

'I thought you might be homesick, so I've had a go at some traditional British food.'

'Wow,' was all Suzannah could think of to say when she saw it and everything looked perfectly cooked.

'I asked an old English friend of mine to e-mail me some suggestions for what you might like and they kindly forwarded me the Yorkshire pudding recipe.'

'Dante, it's delicious.' She almost told him that she didn't think she'd ever tasted anything so wonderful, but somehow stopped herself. Suzannah recognised her controlled guard was melting fast.

Dante beamed, as he saw the obvious enjoyment Suzannah had in eating the roast dinner. The hard physical exercise in the fresh air sharpened Suzannah's appetite and she tucked in heartily.

'You were saying something earlier about wine,' said Dante.

'Oh yes, I had an idea for the southern part of the estate, the land is very sloping, but gets a lot of sun. I wondered about turning it into a vineyard. That's why I wanted a soil analysis. I don't know if the land and climate are suitable.'

'I've heard this before. You're not going to believe this, but Mr Di Stefano wondered the same thing some time ago. Your predecessor was daunted by the idea and of how much work it would be and left. We didn't say anything to you, as we didn't want to frighten you off.'

'Well that's settled then. There is still a lot of general tidying up to do and the trees on the estate need some attention. I'll need some ladders to do that.'

'There are some in the garage. That all sounds well and good, but you must promise me one thing.'

'What's that?' asked Suzannah.

'When you go up the trees, you make sure either myself or Angela are around.'

'That won't be . . . '

' . . . Listen to me, Suzannah,' interrupted Dante. 'This estate is very isolated. If you had a fall and both myself or Angela were away, there wouldn't be anyone who could help you.'

Suzannah nodded her head. 'You're right. I'm sorry. That's very sensible. I'll take care.'

'Good,' said Dante, as he topped up her wine.

'I'll also do some work into looking into how feasible grape growing is around here.'

'I know a few wine growers in the region, I'll let you have a list of names, it might be worth you making some calls, you might get some good advice about which varieties of grape are suitable.'

'You think they'll talk to me and not think I'm competition?'

'I shouldn't think so. The land isn't huge, by wine growers' standards, so we would only be a small-scale operation. Besides, Mr Di Stefano is very well known around here. If you say who you work for, there shouldn't be any problem.'

Suzannah nodded, feeling budding excitement at the idea, tinged with sadness that she would never see her plans to fruition.

By now, Suzannah and Dante had finished their meal and Suzannah felt contentedly full.

'Hope you've got room for some

dessert,' said Dante, 'it's only very light.'

'Just a small portion please. What is it?' asked Suzannah.

'Freshly made ice-cream with strawberries. I'll confess right now that Angela made the ice-cream.'

Suzannah smiled. 'Let me help you with the plates.'

'No, please. I'd rather you stayed out of the kitchen. I know if you see it, you'll want to help clear up and I'd rather you didn't.'

'Whyever not?' asked Suzannah.

'Because I want you to relax. This is my peace offering after I overreacted the other day. Besides, you've been toiling away all day and need a rest. Angela said so and I never argue with Angela.'

'Wise man,' said Suzannah, raising her eyebrows.

'Now, you just stay where you are and I'll bring through dessert.'

Dante described the strawberries and ice-cream in such a casual way,

Suzannah wasn't expecting the beautifully presented treat. The ice-cream wasn't ice-cream: it was its mouth-watering Italian cousin, gelato. Made with real vanilla, with fresh, exquisitely sweet strawberries that were lightly scented with rosewater.

★   ★   ★

During dinner, the storm gradually receded, as Suzannah and Dante's conversation flowed. Both were relaxed and happy.

After dessert, Suzannah went into the lounge, while Dante made some coffee. 'Sounds like the storm's coming round again,' said Dante, as he passed Suzannah a cup of coffee.

'I bet the view from the bell tower's fabulous right now,' said Suzannah, a little wistfully.

'Do you want to go up there, now?' said Dante. He knew the answer at once. Suzannah's eyes lit up at the thought.

'Ok, we'll need to go through the kitchen, but I want you to promise to keep your eyes closed until you get to the bottom of the bell tower stairs. I don't want you to see the mess in there.'

'Don't be silly Dante, if I keep my eyes closed, I'll fall over something and then there really be a terrible mess. Look, I won't look left or right, just forward. What else can I do?'

'Let me lead you.'

'What?' said Suzannah, laughing.

When they reached the kitchen door, Dante urged Suzannah to close her eyes and he held her hand and led her gently through the kitchen. This was the first time Dante had touched Suzannah and the electricity between them was palpable. Suzannah felt it instantly and wondered if Dante did too.

After taking a few tentative steps into the kitchen, Dante stopped.

'Are we there yet?' asked Suzannah.

'No, but you can open your eyes,' replied Dante.

Suzannah opened her eyes to see a chocolate cake on the kitchen table, beautifully iced with the words, 'Welcome Suzannah' across the top.

'Don't look at me, it was all Angela's doing,' said Dante. Suzannah wasn't so sure. Although Dante had done a fantastic impression of being a bumbling chef, his delicious results betrayed his obvious culinary skill.

'It's beautiful! You know Dante, I have a feeling you're always full of surprises.'

Dante's expression darkened slightly and Suzannah instantly noticed. 'Well, I don't like to be predictable,' he said at last.

'Do you want some now or are you too full?'

'I don't think I can resist. I know, why don't we go up the bell tower and watch the storm, like we said. After climbing all those steps, we'll have worked off enough dinner to manage some cake,' said Suzannah. Dante nodded and smiled in agreement.

The view from the top of the bell tower was every bit as breathtaking this time as the last. Suzannah looked out across the lake, the surging wind blowing her long hair across her face. Dante moved towards her and gently moved it away and kissed her tenderly.

Suzannah responded, put her arms around him and kissed back. The tenderness turned to passion. A large crack of thunder, suddenly brought Suzannah to her senses and she pulled away, as the knowledge of Dante's secret flooded her memory once more.

'I'm sorry,' said Dante. Suzannah couldn't look at him and she turned away looking out across the navy blue expanse in front of her, tears streaming down her eyes. She watched the lightening, which would momentarily clarify the darkness and the tumultuous lake was revealed; its state of profound turmoil echoed Suzannah's heart, as clearly as a mirror.

'Suzannah, there's something I should tell you. I've been hiding something from you and I want you to know . . . '

' . . . Shhh. Don't tell me Dante. Whatever it is, I don't want to know, I know you have secrets. I need to think.'

'But, Suzannah, you don't understand . . . '

7

Suzannah didn't stay to listen and ran back down the steps. After a couple of minutes, she waited a moment. Silence.

Relieved that Dante wasn't following her, she continued a little more steadily and at the foot of the steps, deliberately didn't look at the cake and went straight up to her room and locked the door.

At once, Suzannah knew what had happened. In that one kiss, both she and Dante knew their feelings for one another and she ached as she realised he was about to confess his thieving intent to her.

She had already made up her mind to trap him and turn him in once he made his move on Mr Di Stefano's sculpture collection and now that task was that much harder.

How can I have fallen in love so

quickly, she asked herself. This wasn't typical of her usual level-headedness. Dante had captured her heart and now with sadness, she firmed her resolve to catch him, as a thief.

After all, she thought, if he could betray his friend and employer Mr Di Stefano, he could betray her one day.

Trying not to give way to waves of tears, Suzannah wondered what to do. She half expected a knock at the door, but it never came and eventually she fell asleep, exhausted, while lying on top of the bed, still clothed, with a stripe of mascara across her tear-stained cheek.

★ ★ ★

The next morning, Suzannah woke up with a start on hearing the birds in the trees and quickly looked at her clock, fearing she had overslept. On seeing it was only 7 a.m., she sighed with relief and got up and went straight to the bathroom to take a shower.

'Yuk!' She exclaimed on seeing her

face in the mirror and Suzannah quickly cleansed her face, trying to remember if she had ever gone to bed before without washing her face.

Dante, she said to herself. Knowing she had fallen in love with him, without intending to, she tried to talk herself out of it. She knew that his affection might be expedient in light of his plans.

If I'm in love with him, it is easier for him to make me a willing scapegoat. Unless . . . She thought hard, hoping to think of a more innocent explanation for what she overheard that night.

It was with great sadness, she realised she couldn't think of one innocent explanation for anything she heard that night. Nothing. Dante was a thief, of that she was certain.

When she returned from the bathroom, Suzannah noticed a note pinned to her door. She wasn't sure if had just been put there, or if she didn't notice it before. The writing looked familiar and she tore it open.

Dear Suzannah,

Mr Di Stefano called late last night and I've had to leave early this morning on business. I will be away for a few days, so you will have the place to yourself for a while. It's probably as well, I apologise for last night. I think you know my feelings for you, now. I'm sorry it isn't reciprocated. Don't worry, please don't fear me, you don't have to leave.

I will keep out of your way, unless you specifically need me for something. I'll leave the greenhouses in your capable hands and do what you think best with the rest of the estate.

While I'm away, I would very much appreciate it if you would stay at the house every night and keep an eye on things. It won't always be like this, within the next couple of weeks, I will have finished upgrading the security for the estate. Take care.

Dante.

Suzannah was both relieved, yet saddened on learning of Dante's departure. Relieved in that she needed space to think, but saddened, because despite everything, she loved being with him and his note sounded to her so final and resigned.

When Suzannah finally went downstairs, she was surprised to see Angela. 'You're early,' said Suzannah.

'Dante asked if I'd come in early, I think he was a bit worried about you for some reason, wouldn't say why.'

'Where is he?'

'He's gone to the airport, you've only just missed him. He's gone to check over the security arrangements for the tour.'

'Tour? What tour?' asked Suzannah.

'Don't you know? Mr Di Stefano's sculpture collection is going to London, for a major public exhibition. The sculptures are flying out in a week and Dante's gone out with an insurance man to make sure the security is up to scratch.'

'I see,' said Suzannah. Trying not let the full implications of this knowledge show on her face, Suzannah drank her coffee in silence, declining a pastry.

'Go on, just have one. You can't go and do manual work on an empty stomach,' said Angela.

'No, really. I ate well last night.'

'You two had an argument didn't you,' said Angela.

'Did Dante tell you?'

'He didn't have to. Your cake hasn't been cut. By the looks of things, I'd guess you two fell out sometime shortly after dessert.'

'You'd make a fantastic detective, Angela,' said Suzannah. 'Where is the cake?'

'Don't you worry, I've put it in a tin for you. It's on the kitchen table so you can have a slice anytime you like. Would you like some now?'

Suzannah thought for the moment, strangely, although she couldn't stomach a pastry, she really wanted to try that cake.

'Yes please, but just a small slice.' Angela beamed.

'I'll get you another coffee to go with it.'

The cake was light and moist and contained large chunks of chocolate. Suzannah had never tasted such a lovely cake.

'Angela, this wonderful. You really are an excellent cook.'

'What's it got to do with me?' this was all Dante's doing. He's actually a very good cook, but he doesn't let on.'

'You mean he made this himself?'

'Certainly did.'

'What about the minestrone soup?'

'Nothing to do with me. Whatever Dante cooked for you last night was completely his own doing.'

More lies. Why couldn't he just tell me he was a fantastic cook?

While watering the plants, Suzannah realised she'd have to be on full alert as the sculptures were travelling abroad in a week's time.

Dante or his associates would almost

certainly make their move on the artwork within that time frame.

Realising she needed time to think, she got her sketch pad and started to sketch some of the orchids, partly as a preparatory step in thinking of ideas for a clay sculpture, but mainly, as when drawing, Suzannah found she could think clearly and right now she needed a carefully thought out plan.

Suzannah sketched quickly, her pencil darting rapidly across the page, her thoughts churning in her mind. In order to be sure of protecting Mr Di Stefano's collection, Suzannah decided to sleep in the study during Dante's absence, guarding the hidden entrance to the cellar.

Dante knew the burglar alarm system and Suzannah therefore assumed the burglars would also know the security codes.

One thing they wouldn't anticipate was to see Suzannah in the study, armed with the gun and prepared to use it.

The first part of her emerging plan, Suzannah decided to put into action that same evening, after Angela had left for the day. She wanted to make sure that the study was the only entrance to the hidden cellar, if not, then her plans to save the artwork would be thwarted.

Suzannah also resolved to learn how to use the handgun in Dante's desk drawer, in a desperate moment, it could save her life.

After an hour's sketching, Suzannah was clear about what she had to do and tried to put her thoughts of her plan aside for the day and went outside to clear scattered branches that had been wrenched from the trees in the storm.

Suzannah eyed the trees near to the greenhouses with some concern, she knew they needed some maintenance work in the very near future. One old elm in particular seemed to have a branch that might be damaged and if it fell would break through one of the greenhouse roofs.

At lunchtime, Suzannah went indoors

and Angela made her a sandwich and gave her another slice of cake.

'Angela, do you know when Dante will be back?'

'He didn't say, do you need to speak to him?'

'It's nothing urgent, but if you hear from him, will you let me know.'

'Will do, now eat your sandwich.'

8

In the afternoon, Suzannah tidied up the trees in the area surrounding the greenhouses. Angela held the ladder and insisted on staying with her, for safety's sake. Although, Suzannah was grateful for Angela's help, she longed for some time alone.

The events of the last twenty-four hours had taken their toll, but the concentration needed to complete her work, helped her gain some perspective from her feelings.

At six o'clock, Suzannah went back to the greenhouses and then called it a day. Back at the house, Angela had already gone and as much as she liked the housekeeper, was glad to have some time alone. Suzannah made some coffee and cut a slice of cake and ate it looking out of the window.

Hearing the phone, Suzannah turned

to answer it, but hesitated and considered letting it ring out, but realised it might be important and eventually picked it up.

'Mac! How are you?'

'Fine, how are you? And how's the job.'

'Oh I'm fine and I love the work,' said Suzannah, talking in only vague terms about her new job. She didn't want to explain things to Mac; she suspected he still had feelings for her and was therefore reluctant to explain that she had fallen head over heals in love with someone she had good reason to believe was an art thief. Besides, the work itself was brilliant.

'Anyway, I've got some good news. I've a touring exhibition coming up, from Germany, through Switzerland and ending in Milan.'

'Oh Mac, that's fantastic!' said Suzannah. She was genuinely glad for her friend, but wasn't surprised at his success, she knew he was outstanding.

'It's all set for the beginning of

autumn and I was wondering . . . '

' . . . Go on,' urged Suzannah.

'Well I wondered if your new employers could spare you for a couple of weeks in the autumn. I'd really appreciate your help, with your knowledge of Italian and everything.'

'Mac, I'd be delighted to. I'll certainly do it.'

'Don't you need to ask Mr Stefano first?'

'Mac, don't worry about it, whatever happens I'll help you with your exhibition. And in the meantime, if you need my help, just fax or email any letters you need translating.'

'You're a star,' said Mac. And he meant it.

Talking to Mac, lifted Suzannah's spirits and after a brief shower, she made herself a light tomato pasta dish and then went into the study and lifted the trap door to the cellar.

With a torch, she quickly descended the cellar steps, switched on the light and felt along the wall, checking for any concealed entrances to the cellar. There didn't seem to be any and she returned to the study, before going outside to check for any hidden entrances.

There were none, and Suzannah was fairly sure that the only way into the large cellar safe was through the study.

Suzannah set the burglar alarms, brought down an alarm clock, a duvet from her room into the study, then made some tea and settled in for the night. The study had a lot of books about sculpture and orchids and Suzannah looked forward to a long evening reading.

Remembering she needed a weapon, Suzannah opened the desk drawer; the handgun was still in its place. Suzannah touched it, but couldn't quite bring herself to pick it up and closed the drawer and stood up to choose a book.

After browsing for at least fifteen minutes, Suzannah at last settled on reading a biography of one of her favourite sculptors: The Swiss-Italian, Alberto Giacometti and read happily for several hours, before fatigue blurred the words and she reluctantly put the book down. With a yawn, Suzannah set her alarm and went to sleep on the floor.

After what seemed like only a few minutes, Suzannah's alarm clock went off and she looked at it realising she had slept surprisingly well. Suzannah got up quickly and swiftly returned her things to her room; she wanted all evidence of her sleeping in the study gone by the time Angela arrived.

At that time, Suzannah didn't want to share any of her suspicions with anyone, even Angela. She could tell the woman was in awe of Dante and couldn't trust her not to tell him of her concerns.

While freshening up in the bathroom, Suzannah heard Angela arrive and went downstairs for breakfast.

'You're early aren't you, Angela?'

'Well, I don't really have set hours. As long as everything's done, Mr Di Stefano doesn't really mind when I come and go. Anyway, I wanted to make sure I was here early in case you were planning on climbing trees again.'

'That's very kind of you, but really, you don't need to worry. I promised Dante that I wouldn't do any of that unless either you or he were around to help, so please don't feel you have to get here specially early for my sake.'

'That's good. You know, you look a little pale, Suzannah, are you well?'

'I'm fine, really,' said Suzannah, as brightly as she could.

'What time did you finish up last night. I hope it wasn't too late.'

'I can't remember exactly, but it was around tea-time.'

'Good. I don't want you working yourself into the ground.'

'Don't worry, Angela. I'm used to physical work. I enjoy it.'

'Still it does have its advantages, your job; I wish I was half as slim as you.'

'Don't say that or I'll start you out doing some gardening,' teased Suzannah.

Angela laughed, 'maybe I'll stick to housekeeping, now let me get you some coffee.'

★ ★ ★

After breakfast, Suzannah went out to the greenhouses, then, with Angela holding the ladder, did some more tidying up of the trees on the estate until lunchtime.

Angela had agreed to spare Suzannah two hours every morning to help with the trees, until all the trees were trimmed. The estate didn't have many trees and Suzannah estimated it would only take a week to sort everything out. After then, the only work they would need for a while, would be tending to storm damage.

In the early afternoon, it started to rain quite heavily and Suzannah decided to spend the time in the study, researching grape varieties on the internet and writing some letters to Mr Di Stefano's wine-growing neighbours.

Very soon, Suzannah found some interesting websites and absorbed herself in learning about grape varieties for several hours.

Around four o'clock, Angela put her head around the study door.

'Hi Angela, do you need me out of the way to clean?'

'No, I don't do this room. Dante prefers to do it himself. Anyway, I'm done for the day. Do you need anything before I go?'

'No, I'm fine, thanks. Have a good evening.'

After Angela left, Suzannah thought about what she had said. She was surprised Dante didn't let her clean the study and wondered for the first time if he might mind herself using the study while he was away.

Suzannah then concluded it was obvious why Angela wasn't allowed to clean in there: she would pull back the rug to vacuum or mop the floor and uncover the hidden cellar entrance. It made perfect sense that as few people learn about that as possible.

With me using the computer it would be very unlikely I found the entrance by accident. And Suzannah gave the matter no further thought, spending the evening in much the same way as the previous one, reading, once the orchids had been tended to.

★　★　★

The following day was unusual in that Angela phoned early on to say she wouldn't be coming in that day, because of an illness in the family. As it was raining heavily, Suzannah decided to spend the day researching grape varieties and making some phone calls.

She was surprised at how welcoming Dante's contacts had been and soon made several appointments for the following week to look round some local vineyards.

After eating her evening meal, Suzannah looked out of the window on to a clear starlight night and a hunter's moon. I bet the view from the bell tower is fantastic, she thought and went up there to look out on to the lake.

It was breathtakingly beautiful, clear midnight blue, with silvery highlights from the sky. It was a haunting image one which Suzannah wished to fix in her mind.

She stood there absorbed in the sight before her for some time. Eventually, however, her thoughts returned to Dante and of the night he kissed her. Suzannah's heart ached with the memory. For a moment, she almost believed he was behind her again, about to touch her.

My mind's playing tricks on me, she thought, but turned round anyway and wondered if she imagined a movement from the stairway. Of course I didn't and shook her head before returning her attention to the lake once more, a tear escaping down her cheeks.

After a couple more minutes, Suzannah sighed and went back down the steps, trying to drive thoughts of Dante from her mind. It wasn't easy, she tried reading, but even the book about Giacometti failed to absorb her, as it had last night. Still thoughts of Dante kept intruding and of what might have been. I won't let my feelings stop me from doing what I have to do, she said to herself.

Finding her concentration lacking, Suzannah went to the lounge and watched a film on TV for a couple of hours, before returning to the study, feeling a little calmer.

Suzannah heard a rumble of thunder and looked at the clock, it was 11:45 and another storm was clearly brewing. As she didn't feel at all sleepy, Suzannah went back up the bell tower to watch the impending storm over the lake. The scene was a dramatic contrast to the security of the lake only a couple of hours previously.

Suddenly, Suzannah saw a flicker of light from the corner of her eye. Oh no! Not again, she strained in the distance towards the north edge of the estate

— where it borders woodland and waited. She didn't wait long, soon she saw the flash of a torch beam. They're already in the grounds!

Suzannah raced down the steps and checked the burglar alarm was activated, then rushed to the study and closed the door. It had a lock and she quickly turned the key and put a chair against the door. Then, taking a deep breath, Suzannah opened the desk drawer and took out the gun, wishing she'd spent some time in learning how to use it.

There was a cartridge next to it and Suzannah quickly found where it slotted in and assumed correctly that this was how to load it. Suzannah knew that as soon as the burglar alarm sounded the police would soon be on their way.

A realisation hit Suzannah and she suddenly felt a sense of dread. Of course the burglar alarm won't go off, they already know the code from Dante! Trying not to let fear grip her,

Suzannah listened instead for sounds within the house. It came soon enough and Suzannah quickly picked up the phone to dial the police, but there was no ringtone. The phone line had been cut off.

Suzannah sat in a study chair facing the door and picked up the gun. She felt around every edge, locating the safety catch — a button on the nozzle and pressed it. She hoped that would be enough to make it work.

Someone tried the study door, then rattled it. A thought occurred to Suzannah, there was just a small chance it was Mr Di Stefano or Dante returning.

'Who's there?' she called. There was no reply. Somehow she knew there wouldn't be. The rattling stopped for a moment and Suzannah knew that the thieves would either be scared off by knowing she was in there or their resolve would harden.

A moment later there was thumping at the door, someone was pushing their shoulder against it. Hard. The lock wasn't reinforced, more like the kind found on a bathroom door and Suzannah knew that in only a few moments she would be confronting a professional gang of thieves. Although terrified, she grasped the gun firmly and retreated to behind the desk.

The door gave way and three masked men appeared. 'Put your hands in the air or I'll shoot,' said Suzannah, as resolutely as she could. 'Don't listen to her, she's just the gardener, she doesn't know how to use that thing,' said one of the men.

The voice wasn't familiar and neither were any of the men. Certainly none of them were tall enough to be Dante.

Suzannah knew she had to prove she was serious and only had a few seconds to do so and was moments away from one of them lunging at the gun, putting her in a perilous situation.

One of the men moved towards her and she pointed the gun at his legs and fired. The sound was explosive and

Suzannah nearly dropped the gun in surprise. A moment later, two of the men ran away leaving the other lying on the floor, bleeding from a leg wound.

The sounds of the men retreating were interrupted by a scuffling sound and Suzannah went out into the hall to see what was going on.

'On the floor were the two men and Dante.'

'Stop where you are or I'll shoot,' said Suzannah. The two masked men stood up slowly and Dante dusted himself down and moved towards Suzannah.

'And you,' said Suzannah firmly.

'Surely you don't think . . . ' Dante's expression changed. He lifted his hands slowly. 'Look you're making a mistake, I just rugby tackled them to the ground.'

'They're your gang, Dante. Don't try to fool me. Why else were you here. You're supposed to be in London,' said Suzannah pointing the gun at Dante, with tears streaming down her face.

'I can explain all that, but first we

need to get the police here and an ambulance.'

'The phone wires have been cut,' said Suzannah.

'No problem, if you let me put my hands down, I have my mobile.' Suzannah hesitated.

'Suzannah, you have to trust me on this.'

'Did you shoot someone in the study?'

'Yes, but only in the leg,' said Suzannah.

'He could still die unless we get an ambulance here quickly. Unless you let me make that call, how are we going to get the police here?' Suzannah looked in Dante's eyes, searching for the truth.

'OK, make the call, but do it in front of me.' Suzannah kept the gun pointing at Dante and she could see the hurt in his face, which he made no attempt to hide. Dante slowly reached inside his pocket and brought out his mobile.

'Why don't you phone, then you

know the call's really been made,' said Dante sadly.

Suzannah nodded. Very slowly, Dante bent down, put the phone on the floor and gently kicked it towards Suzannah.

'Now while you make that call, I'm going to help the man in the other room, he's bleeding and needs help, now. Will you trust me on this?' Suzannah nodded and let him past her.

'You keep an eye on those two,' he said, indicating the two masked men, still standing with their hands up.

Suzannah made the call to the police, while Dante stemmed the bleeding in the leg of the shot man. When he'd done what he could, he came back into the hall, Suzannah took a deep breath.

'You better take this,' Suzannah said handing Dante the gun. 'I trust you.'

Realising she was trusting him with her life, Suzannah knew if he really was part of a ruthless gang, he could shoot her before the police arrived and the gang would cover for him.

Deep down, she now knew he was

innocent. Although there was a lot about this episode she didn't understand, she realised Dante wasn't part of the gang. The hurt in his eyes when she pointed the gun wasn't faked. He didn't seem at all frightened, only deeply sad and hurt.

'You're taking a risk, aren't you giving me this,' said Dante.

'Yes, I trust you, I'm betting my life on it.' Suzannah saw a flicker of relief in Dante's face and he smiled for the first time.

Seeing Dante and Suzannah distracted, one of the two men lunged forward and punched Suzannah in the jaw. She felt immediately dizzy and at once, her vision blurred. In the few seconds before she lost consciousness, she saw the same man grappling with Dante for the gun. Then her vision went black, but before she passed out completely she heard a shot being fired.

'Dante,' she murmured under her breath, before she collapsed, wondering if Dante was still alive.

9

Suzannah woke up to hear the paramedics calling her name. She lifted her head from the floor and looked around, a surge of dread crawled down her back when she didn't see Dante.

'Dante,' she called out, clearly distressed.

'Dante's fine, now don't you worry,' said the paramedic, trying to shine a torch in her eyes to look at her pupil size. Suzannah pushed him away and sat up.

'I'm all right. Where's Dante?' The two paramedics looked at each other.

'The same as you, he pushed us away as well. Don't worry, he's fine. He's giving a statement to the police now.'

'Just before I lost consciousness, I heard a shot . . . '

' . . . It's all right. A shot was fired in the tussle for the gun, but fortunately, the bullet went into the wall. No-one's dead.'

Just then Dante appeared in the doorway and rushed to hug Suzannah. 'Are you all right?' he asked.

'I'm fine, but what about you? Dante, I thought you were dead.' The strain and confusion of the events suddenly overwhelmed Suzannah and she sobbed uncontrollably. Dante folded his arms around her and held her tight.

The effects of the punch were still apparent and Suzannah suddenly felt dizzy. 'Suzannah. Suzannah, answer me!' Dante noticed at once Suzannah was still dazed and she heard him ordering a paramedic to look at her. Now everything seemed remote and distant, dreamlike even. But Suzannah felt deeply happy, knowing Dante was OK and taking charge.

When Suzannah next woke up, she saw Dante, looking at her a little anxiously. 'I'm glad you're here,' said Suzannah. Dante squeezed her hand.

'So am I,' said Dante.

'Am I in hospital?'

'Yes, but don't worry, you've already had a brain scan and have got a clean bill of health. The doctors think you are just a little concussed. You should be fine in a few days but you'll have to take it easy for a while.'

'No climbing trees then,' said Suzannah.

Dante raised his eyebrows. 'Definitely no climbing trees! Don't worry, you can convalesce back home and take as long as you like.' Dante's use of the word home felt comforting.

'Thanks,' said Suzannah, managing a weak smile. 'I guess you've given Angela strict instructions to fuss over me and stop me doing any work on the estate for a bit.' Suzannah at once noticed Dante's expression alter. She knew he was hiding something.

'What is it?' said Suzannah, trying to sit up.

'You just relax. I'm going to take care of you. Angela doesn't work for us any more. Now don't worry about it and try

131

and get some rest.'

'Dante, I want to know. There's a lot of what's gone on I don't understand. Please don't shield me.' Dante nodded.

'I've a lot of explaining to do but I would rather do it in private, once I've taken you back home. I think we've a lot to talk about and I can't really put you in the picture until we've talked.'

Suzannah nodded. She could hear the conversation in the next cubicle clearly and she knew she and Dante had a lot to talk about and he was right. This wasn't the place. 'OK, that's fine, but please just briefly tell me about Angela.'

'One of the masked men, the one I shot, was her brother. She was a plant, feeding information about the estate to her brother who planned to steal the sculptures. I've suspected for a while but things came to a head before I could prove anything.'

Trying to take everything in, Dante and Suzannah were interrupted by the nurse coming to take Suzannah's blood pressure and look at her pupil size.

'Ah! You're awake. How are you feeling?' said the nurse.

'I'm fine. When can I go home?' replied Suzannah quickly. The nurse looked at Dante, who said, 'If she's medically stable, I can guarantee that once she is discharged she is going to get plenty of rest. Aren't you, Suzannah?' said Dante teasingly.

'Well, if your observations stay stable for the rest of the day and overnight, I don't see why you shouldn't be able to go tomorrow. I'll have to check with the doctor but you were lucky not to break your jaw after that punch.'

★　★　★

After the nurse left, Suzannah leaned over to Dante. 'Take me home tomorrow, regardless. I promise I'll be good and rest.' Before they had a chance to say anything further, they noticed the nurse gesture towards Dante, pointing to her watch. Clearly visiting time was over.

'Ah well, you need rest,' said Dante.

'I suppose so,' replied Suzannah, sadly.

'Suzannah?'

'Yes?'

'I love you.' Suzannah beamed and reached across to hug Dante.

'I love you, too.'

★   ★   ★

For the rest of the day, Suzannah tried not to think too hard about all the things she didn't understand. She knew Dante would explain everything soon and she was so relieved he wasn't a thief after all. Also, she knew if she dwelt on things, it might raise her blood pressure and she didn't want that or she wouldn't be allowed home the following day.

Later on, Suzannah saw a doctor who agreed that if her observations remained stable overnight, she could go home the following day after the morning ward round, which in practice would mean around lunchtime.

Dante rang in the evening to see how she was and arranged to pick her up. He also apologised for not coming to see her that evening. He was tied up until after visiting hours, finishing giving his statement to the police.

That night, before she went to sleep, Suzannah could hardly contain her excitement at going back and really felt that a new chapter in her life was beginning, one that included Dante. Suzannah slept well.

The next morning, Suzannah felt considerably better and the doctors were happy for her to go home as long as she rested for a couple of weeks. Packing her bag, the nurse asked her about her arrangements for going home.

'Do you need us to book you a taxi?'

'No, that's all right. Dante's picking me up.'

'Ah, yes, Mr Di Stefano has been

very attentive to you, hasn't he?' said the nurse with a twinkle in her eye.

Suzannah turned to look at her directly. 'Attentive? Mr Di Stefano? But I've only met him once, it's Dante who's been attentive.'

'Yes, Dante. Dante Di Stefano,' said the nurse, perplexed at Suzannah's reply.

At once, understanding hit Suzannah with more force than the punch she previously endured. 'Dante,' she muttered under her breath.

When the nurse had finally gone, Suzannah quickly went to the phone and called Mac, quickly filling him in on the extraordinary events of the last few weeks and asked him to call her back once he'd done a little detective work.

When she finished the call, Suzannah found the nurse. 'I know this is an unusual request but a friend of mine needs to send me some information urgently. Would you mind if he used your fax number?'

The nurse didn't mind and within an hour the anticipated document arrived. Mac had been on the Internet and found a couple of press cuttings with pictures of Mr Di Stefano whose first name was indeed Dante. Two of the articles included a photograph and although the picture quality was poor, there was no mistaking the identity.

He lied to me! He said he was Dante Candurro. Suzannah at once understood that the person introduced to her as Mr Di Stefano was probably the real Dante Candurro.

How could he let me think he was someone else all this time! Suzannah was tearful and wondered what other secrets lay behind Dante's brooding expression.

When Dante arrived to pick Suzannah up, he knew after one glance that she knew who he was.

'Who told you?'

'The nurse. I didn't quite believe her at first and did some detective work,' said Suzannah, handing the fax to

Dante as she got into the car.

'I don't know you at all, Dante. You've lied to me. You hid your identity, you didn't tell me about Angela, although I assume you got her to lie to me about who you were as well. And you haven't explained to me why you were planning to have your own collection stolen. Was it for the insurance money?'

'What? Planning to have the artwork stolen? Whatever gave you that idea?'

'I overheard you talking to someone, one stormy night. I didn't hear everything but I understood enough. That's why I pointed the gun at you the other night.'

'I can explain . . . '

' . . . I bet you can,' said Suzannah. 'I'm sure you've an answer for everything. I must admit I need to hear this, but I should tell you at once I've heard your explanation. I don't intend to stay one more night under your roof. I feel betrayed Mr Di Stefano.'

10

Once back at the house, Dante sat Suzannah down and tried to explain hat had happened.

'When I first met you at the gallery, I fell for you straightaway.'

'Love at first sight?' said Suzannah, sarcastically.

'Yes,' replied Dante, ignoring her tone. 'On impulse I introduced myself as my personal assistant that night because I needed to get to know you. The truth is, Suzannah, rich people attract gold diggers. I needed to be sure you'd love me for myself and not because I'm the infamous Dante Di Stefano.'

'So employing me was a charade, just to get to know me, to play with me. What if you decided you didn't like me, would I have got fired?'

'No,' said Dante firmly. 'I wanted to

keep my feelings in check until I was sure, both of myself and of your feelings. If things hadn't worked out, I intended to judge you solely on your work and you would have been none the wiser.'

'How would you explain your identity?'

'I would have told you I did it, to be able to evaluate your work and personality at close quarters, without intimidating you, with the view to promoting you. You see, I really do need someone in my employ whom I can trust to manage my artwork.

'Dante Candurro, the man you were introduced to as myself that night at the gallery is excellent with orchids and business matters in general, but his knowledge is limited with respect to sculpture. I couldn't send him round to the major galleries of the world, buying up artwork which I hadn't seen, on my behalf.'

Suzannah thought about this a moment. 'I see, that makes some sense.

Anyone not steeped in the art world might get duped. At the higher end of the market there are some sharks out there.'

'Exactly . . . '

' . . . But, Dante. I can't get over the feeling that I've been used. A toy at your disposal. I've always been very independent and it feels like a betrayal. I'm not sure I can get over this. I've never lied to you, Dante. Yet, I've fallen in love with you, and I don't even know who you are.'

Dante moved over to put his arm round Suzannah, but she pulled away. 'What other secrets do you hold, Dante?'

'Like what?'

'Like, what were you doing lurking round the grounds at night, talking to someone about stealing your own art collection?'

'The problem when you eavesdrop is you only get part of the story. When you tore down that shrubbery, you high-lighted something true: namely, the security here isn't good enough. I've employed a security firm to look at our security and upgrade it. Part of how they find out how good your security is, is to try and break in at night, and see if the security already in place picks it up.

'By chance, I returned to the house to get some documents and just as I drove through the gates, noticed someone trying to break in and confronted them, established who they were and then we had a hypothetical discussion about how to steal my own artwork. That bit I presume you overheard.'

'It was dark and pouring with rain. Why didn't you talk about it indoors?'

'Because one of the stipulations of the company is that while the security of any estate is being upgraded, no employees are informed of it. It's not that I didn't trust you, but Mr Beckman, who runs the company, wouldn't have talked about it while you were around. They make the assumption that employees tend to eavesdrop.'

Suzannah blushed slightly. 'I was

only trying to protect your sculpture collection. I hate these gangs of art thieves who steal things just for a private owner, with the artwork being lost to the world forever. I didn't want to see that happen to the Di Stefano collection.'

'I knew that, Suzannah and I appreciate your efforts and your raw courage. I can't imagine how much bravery it took to confront those burglars the other night, but how did you know they would be coming that particular night? And how did you find out I kept the sculptures here?'

Suzannah felt a little embarrassed, as she related her snooping, finding the hidden cellar entrance in the study.

'I knew the collection was due to go to the UK on tour soon so I guessed the thieves would make their move within a couple of days and as I had the place to myself, I slept in the study until they came. Anyway, where did you spring from that night? I thought you were in London.'

'I told Angela that. The security company did a security check on yourself and Angela and they came up with some information that made us suspect her. I didn't really go to London, their security is excellent. I didn't need to check it out myself. Instead, I spent the nights in the garage, on watch, in case they tried to break in.'

'Where were you in the day?' asked Suzannah.

'I slept in a hotel. I knew they were unlikely to make a move in broad daylight.'

'Why didn't you have some back-up?'

'Usually I did, except on the night in question. A private bank that used this company for security had had a tip-off that there was to be a raid that night. The police were there but this firm drafted in all available men for one night. Ironically, it was a false alarm.'

'Anyway, where is the real Dante Candurro? I'd like to know where he is as I've fallen in love with him.'

'I sent him off to Brazil, out of the way for a few weeks. He's deep in the jungle, after orchids. Don't worry, he loves that part of his work. But it isn't him you fell for, it was me.'

'I can't live with all these lies, Dante. I'm a straightforward kind of person. I know many girls would do anything to become involved with you and all your money, but I can't be bought. And I don't like the lies, Dante. I would be grateful if you'd book me into a hotel. I don't want to stay here a moment longer. You even tried to deceive me about your cooking!'

Inside, Suzannah's heart was breaking. She still loved Dante and it took all her strength to pull away, but she knew she must pull away. It would be too easy to accept his explanations and go back to being in love, but Suzannah still felt deeply hurt.

'Suzannah. I love you. I know I've hurt you and knowing what I know now, I would change so many things, Please forgive me.'

'Dante, I do forgive you, but I can't love you. I mustn't love you.' Suzannah bit her lip and ran upstairs to her room before tears overwhelmed her.

★ ★ ★

With great sadness Suzannah packed her things and moved out of the house. Leaving her bags in the hall while she waited for a taxi, Suzannah went outside and took one last look at the house, at the lake, at the place she had in such a short time become a part of her.

She hadn't realised it until now, when she was about to leave. Suzannah then looked up at the bell tower and wonder if on that night, Dante really was up there with her, or had she imagined it? I'll never know, she thought to herself.

Suzannah walked towards the greenhouses, but from a distance could see Dante inside, watering the plants and immediately retreated, hoping he hadn't seen her. Her task was hard enough.

She knew that if he petitioned her to stay again, her resolve would weaken.

Hearing the beep of the taxi, Suzannah quickly collected her things and drove off. She tried not to look back but couldn't help it and saw Dante looking sadly after her. 'Goodbye, Dante,' she muttered under he breath, 'I'll always love you.'

Suzannah checked into her small, clean hotel room and tried not to think of how unlike a home it was. She decided to stay in Lugano for a week to fully recover from her injuries, then fly back to the UK. This place had too many painful memories for her to stay here now.

Feeling claustrophobic in her room, Suzannah went out for a walk by the lake and tried to turn her thoughts to the future rather than dwelling on what might have been.

Recent events, however, kept flashing in her mind. Suzannah had never had a broken heart before. In such a short time, Dante had turned her life upside down. Oh, why couldn't he have been Dante Candurro, rather than Mr Dante Di Stefano.

Her conversation with Dante played over and over again in her mind as she walked along the lakeside, hardly noticing her surroundings or the enclosing darkness.

Suddenly a thought struck her with force, stopping her in her tracks. 'Of course!' she exclaimed aloud and suddenly realised Dante was in danger and quite possibly alone at the house.

Suzannah ran back to the hotel as fast as she could and rushed to the phone, hoping he was in. The phone went straight to answer phone. 'Dante. I've no time to explain. You're in danger. Don't phone the security company. I'm coming right over and I'll explain things when I get there.'

★   ★   ★

As soon as she put the phone down, she raced downstairs and asked the desk to call her a cab. By now, the funicular railway was closed and the route by road was long. When she left the house that afternoon, it had taken an hour in the cab to get from Dante's estate to the main town.

'Boat!' said Suzannah out loud as she ran out the hotel door, forgetting about the taxi she'd asked for. Instead, she rushed out towards the lake and looked at the boats which in the daytime ran tourists around the lake. She hoped that just one of these boats was still open for business.

Suzannah's eyes scanned the water-side and she saw a few metres ahead a boat just coming in, dropping off some tourists who had just been for an early evening trip.

'Can I hire you to take me to . . . '

'Sorry, closed for the day. I'm just off home,' interrupted the boatman who was helping the last of the tourists off his boat.

'Please, it's an emergency. A matter of life or death. The journey is only short and you don't have to wait for me. Just drop me off at the mooring on the Di Stefano estate.'

The man was thinking about it and Suzannah offered more money.

'OK, if I don't have to wait for you.'

'No, but I need you to get me there as quickly as you can.'

'No problem, Miss. You'll be there in ten minutes.'

Those ten minutes seemed the longest of her life. Suzannah looked in her bag. She still had the keys to the house. In her turmoil earlier, she had forgotten to leave them, but now was thankful that she had.

If Dante was out, she would need to let herself in. She knew there might well be another attempt to steal Dante's art collection that evening and she had a feeling that they wouldn't mind if Dante was killed if he got in the way.

Once there, Suzannah leaped from the boat on to the mooring and ran up the steep path. It would take her ten minutes of hard running to reach the house this way but she had no other choice.

Suzannah ran hard, ignoring her body's yearning to stop and catch her breath. Her rapid pace paid off though, and when she neared the house, she looked at her watch. It had taken her seven minutes. Looking at the house, she could see a light on and she frantically pressed the bell and to her relief, a familiar figure opened the door.

'Suzannah! You came back.'

'Did you get my message?' said Suzannah.

'Yes, but what's this all about?' said Dante, ushering her in.

'You told me on the night the thieves broke in here your security firm's men were called out on a job which turned out to be a hoax. Right?'

'Right,' said Dante, still not understanding.

'I can't believe it was a coincidence. What if there is a mole in the security firm who planned it that way to make sure you had no back-up that night.'

Dante thought fast. It made sense.

'The thing is, Dante, the collection is leaving soon and if this was part of a large criminal gang, they may well come back. As you shot one of their men, they may also want revenge and I couldn't bear . . . '

Suzannah hesitated, reluctant to say what she felt. 'Dante, I couldn't bear the thought of them harming you and I came to warn you. I tried to phone, but . . . '

' . . . I was in the greenhouses. I go there when I need to think. What you say makes sense. I'll call the police and we'll take it from there.'

Dante picked up the phone and frowned.

'What is it?' said Suzannah.

'The line's been cut off again. Don't worry, I'll call from my mobile.'

Dante made the call quickly, but both knew the gang were already on the estate. Suzannah shuddered as she realised they could have grabbed her if they'd seen her approach.

Even though Dante was able to contact the police, it would probably be some time before they got there as the journey by road from town took some time and Dante and Suzannah both knew it.

Once Dante finished making the call, Suzannah headed off towards the study. 'Where are you going?' said Dante.

'To the study, to guard the cellar entrance, for course.'

'No, not this time, Suzannah. I don't care about the collection enough to risk your life again for it. Quick, follow me.' Dante spoke calmly and firmly and Suzannah followed him upstairs into his private suite.

At once, Suzannah could see why. The door was heavily reinforced and would need a gun to shoot through it. Inside, hanging on the wall, Dante had a gun cabinet which he now unlocked.

'Look and bolt the door,' said Dante as he picked out a rifle and loaded it.

'Suzannah, from now on, stand well away from the door. If they try and shoot through it, I don't want you anywhere near.' Suzannah nodded and went to stand beside Dante.

'I'm sorry you've been dragged into this mess,' said Dante.

'It's not your fault.'

'It is in a way and I'm sorry. Did you come back just to warn me?'

Suzannah looked into Dante's eyes and emotion welled up within her.

'No, not entirely,' said Suzannah.

Dante put the gun down and gently bent forward to kiss her. The feeling overwhelmed Suzannah and she kissed back. They were the love of each other's life and at that moment they knew it.

Abruptly their moment of bliss was interrupted on hearing the burglar alarm. They're in the building. I changed the code so this will give them a jolt.' Dante switched off the light and opened the curtain a little to let in a little moonlight.

A hunter's moon, though Suzannah as she watched Dante pick up the gun and stand between herself and the door.

In the clear moonlight, Suzannah noticed Dante's expression change, the mask came down and now he looked resolute and determined. Although she should have been terrified, Suzannah felt safe. Safe and in love.

11

Outside they heard the sound of running and then a loudspeaker. The police had arrived and they announced that the house was surrounded and for the crooks to come out with their hands up.

'That was fast,' said Dante. 'I didn't expect them for another half hour. 'They must have come by boat, the same as me,' said Suzannah.

Several minutes passed and they strained to hear what was happening. Suzannah moved towards the door.

'Wait!' said Dante. 'We must stay here until we get the all-clear from the police. If they're still in the house and they grab us, they could take us hostage and use us as a bargaining chip.' Suzannah nodded.

Just then, Dante's mobile went off. 'Hello . . . yes . . . we'll be right down.'

Dante put the gun down, turned to Suzannah and gave her a hug.

'We can go down now. They came out with their hands up. They were armed so I think we had a lucky escape. Thank you for coming back, you probably saved my life.'

'I wanted to come back to you, Dante.'

'I let you walk away from me once, Suzannah. I've never felt so broken-hearted as then, I don't intend to let you go again.'

'Good. That's just fine by me,' said Suzannah. 'But I have one condition.'

'Name it, anything,' said Dante without hesitation.

'You never, ever keep anything from me again. No secrets and never try and make out you are anything other than an excellent cook.'

'OK,' said Dante, smiling. 'I only want to share my life you with, Suzannah.'

Dante moved towards Suzannah to kiss her when suddenly they heard the police pounding on the door, asking in an urgent manner if they were all right.

'We're fine,' said Dante.

'I suppose we'd better unlock the door,' said Suzannah.

'What timing!' said Dante, as he slid the bolts back and opened the door to see a group of armed policemen.

By now it was very late and the policemen therefore took the briefest of statements from Dante and Suzannah. Their full statements were to be taken more formally the following day.

There was a short delay while everyone waited for the police vans to arrive. The policemen already at the house had arrived by boat just like Suzannah as it was the fastest way to get to Dante's estate. But the suspects had to be taken away in a van and while waiting for it to arrive, the policemen asked Dante and Suzannah to look at the now handcuffed criminals to see if they recognised anyone.

At once Dante knew one of the men. He was an employee of the security firm he'd hired to upgrade security at the estate. Suzannah's conclusions were correct. This surprised the police, as the firm in question was well known and trusted

★ ★ ★

Within a week, the police made another series of arrests and this time they were sure they had cracked the large criminal network responsible for the plot to steal the Di Stefano art collection and uncovered other stolen treasures in the process. And, at last, Dante and Suzannah felt that they could put this unpleasant episode behind them.

The summer passed idyllically for Suzannah and Dante as they got to know each other fully. Gone was the brooding, mask-like expression, Suzannah first saw in Dante and instead she rarely saw him do anything but smile.

During the time, Suzannah continued her work on the estate. Also, she gradually learned more about Dante's

159

sculpture collection and went on a couple of buying trips overseas on his behalf.

This aspect of her life took an increasing amount of time, leaving her with less time than she would have liked to look after the estate and Dante and Suzannah realised that they would need to hire someone to help with general maintenance

In August, Dante Candurro's younger sister, Gabriella, stayed with them for a couple of weeks. She had just finished her biology degree and was taking some time out deciding how her career should progress.

Suzannah got on very well with Gabriella who gave her a helping hand with the general maintenance of the estate and enjoyed the work very much. So much so, she agreed to take on this work as a job for a few months while she decided what to do next. They frequently chatted in English as Gabriella wanted to improve her language.

October was bright and sunny with the stinging heat of summer over. Autumn was a seemingly perfect time of year in this region. At this time, Suzannah took some time out from her regular work to help Mac with his successful touring exhibition of his work.

'I don't know what I'd have done without you, Suzannah,' said Mac after watching her negotiate the sale of one of his sculptures for double what he thought he could get for it.

'I've had some practice now Dante's put me in charge of his ever-expanding collection. Which reminds me, I think it's time the Di Stefano collection acquired a Mark Mackenzie, don't you?' said Suzannah.

'Take your pick. I mean it. You can have it as a gift,' said Mac. Suzannah put her hand up.

'No, I don't think so, it wouldn't be right to let something go for less than its value. No, I insist we pay you for what it's worth. Besides, I think your work is a good investment, I really do. They'll be worth a fortune in a few years, you see.'

'That would be nice,' said Mac wistfully.

'I've got some news for you,' said Suzannah. Mac thought he knew what that might be, but was surprised by Suzannah's answer.

'The Di Stefano collection's going public full-time. We're going to open a sculpture museum. I really want some of your work there, Mac.'

'Wow! That's a great idea.'

'I think Dante had been thinking about it for some time but just hadn't got round to doing anything abut it.' Suzannah glowed with excitement as she described her plans and Mac was genuinely happy for her. He'd never seen her so happy before. Mac saw two familiar figures approach.

'Ah,' said Mac, 'here come the two Dantes.'

'Hello, Mac,' said Dante Di Stefano

as he put his arm around Suzannah. 'This exhibition is a great success. We've all much to celebrate. Do you know the arrangements for this evening?'

'Yes, thanks. Suzannah's told me the party starts around eight. Is the funicular railway running at that time?'

'No,' said Dante Candurro. It closes at six-thirty. I'll pick you up, if you like?'

'Thanks,' said Mac.

Mac had suspicions that this might not be just any party he was going to and some days ago had taken the precaution of buying a travel iron. He guessed a party at the Di Stefano estate would be an event requiring an ironed shirt and polished shoes at the very least.

Later on, while getting ready for the party, Suzannah sat at her dressing table and put on her ring and moved her hand, watching the diamonds sparkle in the light.

'You look lovely, darling,' said Dante,

bending down behind her to kiss her neck.

'I'm so happy, Dante,' said Suzannah, smiling at him through the mirror.

'So am I. It was a good idea of yours to announce our engagement at a party of friends and relations,' replied Dante, grinning.

'It will be a surprise for some, I know. I suppose I ought to get changed,' said Suzannah, looking at the clock.

'Lovely as you are in just your silk slip and engagement ring, I think perhaps you're right,' said Dante.

★　★　★

Dante Candurro picked up Mac a little early, thus arriving before many of the guests.

Dante quickly introduced him to his sister, one of the few English speakers there that night and the spark between them was instant, just as Suzannah had anticipated.

'How did you know they'd get on?'

said Dante, as he watched Mac and Gabriella chatting and laughing, fully attentive to each other.

Suzannah smiled. 'Intuition. I just had a hunch, like that time when I looked into your eyes and deep down I knew I could trust you even though I didn't understand what was going on.'

Dante kissed Suzannah tenderly on the forehead. 'In that case, I'm very glad you have such fine instincts. What do your instincts tell you now about us?'

'That we'll be very happy together.'

Dante gave Suzannah a hug which was interrupted by clapping and cheers coming from Mac and Gabriella.

'Come on, don't keep us in suspense. When's the wedding?' said Mac with characteristic bluntness.

'How did you know?' said Suzannah.

'Well, other than the fact you're wearing a large diamond on your ring finger, there's something about your permanent wide smile that gave it away. Look, I'm really happy for you both.'

Mac had already guessed the real reason for the party and had a little surprise of his own. When he returned to the UK the following week, he planned to leave one of his sculptures with Suzannah as an early wedding present.

On the other hand, he suddenly considered another possibility as he looked across at Gabriella who was smiling at him. His work was far more popular here than at home. Maybe I should live out here for a while, hmm . . .

THE END

We do hope that you have enjoyed reading this large print book.

Did you know that all of our titles are available for purchase?

We publish a wide range of high quality large print books including:
Romances, Mysteries, Classics
General Fiction
Non Fiction and Westerns

Special interest titles available in large print are:
The Little Oxford Dictionary
Music Book, Song Book
Hymn Book, Service Book

Also available from us courtesy of Oxford University Press:
Young Readers' Dictionary
(large print edition)
Young Readers' Thesaurus
(large print edition)

For further information or a free brochure, please contact us at:
Ulverscroft Large Print Books Ltd.,
The Green, Bradgate Road, Anstey,
Leicester, LE7 7FU, England.
Tel: (00 44) **0116 236 4325**
Fax: (00 44) **0116 234 0205**

Other titles in the
Linford Romance Library:

A STRANGER'S KISS

Rosemary A. Smith

May, 1849. Sara Osborne has received a strange plea for help from her friend Amelia in Cornwall. Concerned, she travels to the imposing cliff-top house of Ravensmount. There, she meets Tobias Tremaine — whom Sara believed to be Amelia's husband. But Tobias claims they never married — and Amelia is missing . . . The mystery deepens as Sara meets Tobias's strange siblings and their father, Abraham. But how does the enigmatic Tamsin fit into the family? What is the secret of Amelia's music box? And will Sara succumb to a stranger's kiss?

RIVALS IN LOVE

Toni Anders

Bryony becomes private secretary to Justin, a charismatic but moody novelist. She finds him attractive — until she meets Rowan, his charming cousin. The two men have been estranged for years since they and Eleanor, whom they both loved, were caught up in a tragedy. Bryony risks Justin's wrath in her attempts to bring about a reconciliation between the cousins. But then she faces a dilemma — which man does she really love? And will history repeat itself?

WINTERHAVEN

Janet Whitehead

Annabel Tyler's boss sent her to the Scottish Highlands to save Winter-haven, the estate of a valued client. But at every turn Annie found a mystery to unravel. Who was David O'Neal, the stranger who seemed to know all about her? What was the dark secret of Winterhaven's deep loch? And were the estate and its inhabitants cursed? But then Annie fell in love with the new master of Winterhaven — and things took an even more dramatic turn!